www.united-pc.eu

JAMES M DYET'S

PETER STEWARTS
MURDER CASES

CASE ONE

THE SERIAL KILLER'S SECRET

My Name Is Peter Stewart

In my first case, I am an Inspector and in the
second I am promoted to Chief Inspector

First Case

The Serial killers Secret

The Legal Profession start to drop like flies through
poisoning my job is to find out why

THE SERIAL KILLER'S SECRET

I could hear the rain lashing against the window pane as I tried to get back to sleep. My alarm clock showed 6.30am and the alarm was set for 6.45am. I really needed that last 15mins before getting ready for work. It felt wonderful as I Snuggled my head into my pillow and started to doze off. A loud bang made me sit upright in bed I put my slippers and dressing gown on and rushed down stairs to the kitchen to investigate. Nothing looked out of place in the kitchen so I looked out of the window, I noticed the dustbin had blown across the yard and hit the back door. Deciding all was ok I started back up the stairs again, as I did I heard my alarm clock go off so I headed back down to make my breakfast.

After my breakfast I started up the stairs when the telephone rang, so back down the stairs again.

"Hello! Oh it's you sergeant, what's up run out of coffee again? Ok I will be there as soon as possible."

That was Sergeant Taylor, A lady has collapsed and died suddenly, the woman was a Miss Harriet May a barrister who lived on her own.

Who am I? I am inspector Peter Stewart. I grabbed a muesli bar and headed off to the scene of the crime.

I arrived at the victim's office to find Sergeant Jack Taylor standing over her body.

"Who found her sergeant and what makes you think its fowl play? It could be just a heart attack!"

"The cleaner phoned for an ambulance and the paramedics phoned us as she appeared to have been poisoned, Miss May was dead when they arrived."

"Where is the cleaner now sergeant? I would like to ask her account of the events."

"She's in the kitchen with Carol, sorry sir I mean constable Forward."

I made my way to the kitchen to find constable Forward and the cleaner sitting at the table sipping mugs of tea. Constable Forward stood up but I told her to stay seated.

"Hello I am inspector Stewart and you are?" The cleaner looked in shock and was crying, she slowly composed her self before saying.

"My name is Mrs. Sandra Green."

"When you are ready I would like you to tell me everything you remember, start from the time you entered the building and up until Miss May's untimely death."

"I arrived here at 6.30am as usual, as I entered I noticed Miss May had come in early as her umbrella was in the lobby and still wet, I called out and she answered from her office on the 1st floor, so I fetched my cleaning equipment from under the stairs then headed upstairs to her office to enquire why she had come in so early. Miss May was sitting at her desk and looked far from happy so I asked if she was ok."

"Was she reading any letters or had she been using the phone? Can you think of any little thing that would point to the reason for her death?"

"If you would stop interrupting I will tell you inspector."

Well that put a red embarrassed glow on my face.

"Sorry I will keep quite; just carry on at your own pace."

I looked at Constable Forward who was grinning all over her face.

"As I was saying, I asked if she was ok and why she was in early as we were good friends and shared our troubles. She remarked that a man had phoned her the evening before; he told her she had ruined his life and he would be getting even. Miss May was a prosecuting Barrister so she made a few enemies and seemed to know who it was. She said she was certain a man she had prosecuted was innocent, even so she had convinced the jury otherwise just to win the case."

"Sorry to interrupt, but did she give any clue to the identity of the man or his crime, anything at all?"

"No but she looked very scared and mentioned that he had seemed a quiet man with warm loving eyes, but as he was taken away from the dock he looked at her, his eyes burned through her cold with hate. She said she still felt repercussions from that man. As she finished that remark she stood up gripping her stomach, screamed in pain and shouted, he's poisoned me. She fell backwards into the chair and onto the floor."

"Did you remove a cup wrapper or anything connected with food or drink from her office or in here?"

"No I haven't touched anything. Perhaps she had something in her handbag or maybe in one of her coat pockets inspector!"

"Good idea Mrs Green, I would like you to accompany me to her office, tell me if you notice anything out of the ordinary."
"I would rather not go back in there while Miss May's body is in there inspector."
"Be better now before the forensic team arrive if you don't mind."

Reluctantly she followed me, being reassured by constable Forward.
We looked on the desk for clues and found nothing to suggest how she had been poisoned. Until the autopsy I can only assume that by the sudden burst of pain and the speed she died, the poison was administered while Mrs Green was present."
Constable Forward searched Mrs. Green along with her cleaning equipment and found nothing; she bagged it all up for the forensic team. The forensics arrived so we all vacated the office; so far Mrs Green was the only suspect. As Mrs Green is the cleaner, her fingerprints and DNA Would be everywhere in the office. The only thing to convict her would be motive. I had no choice but to tell constable Forward to take Mrs green to the station to make a statement and hold her there until further notice.

Back at the station I asked for her phone number so I could inform her husband but she said she was divorced and lived alone. Her husband, daughter and son had never been in trouble with the law and lived miles away. Has Mrs Green told the truth about Mrs May's last words or had she lied to mislead me?

The interrogation proved fruitless and left me baffled to how the poison had entered Miss May, mainly because I was convinced Mrs Green was innocent.
I asked Sergeant Taylor to drive her home. Mrs Green was blond slim and attractive so he jumped at the idea, he had been looking Google eyed at her ever since she was brought in.

By this time it was midday and my stomach was starting to make gurgling sounds, I headed to a café I knew in the next street and ordered a baked potato with cheese and beans and a large black coffee then waited eagerly to get stuck in.
I had eaten half of my dinner when my mobile rang. The call was from Constable Forward asking me to return to the station straight away; another person has been found dead two streets from Miss May's home. Reluctantly I left the rest of my

lunch after having a big gulp of my coffee. I guess that's one of the pitfalls of being on call 24hrs a day.

Constable Forward drove me to the address where we found Sergeant Taylor waiting at the front door. He had responded to the call after dropping Mrs Green off. This time there were no clues at all. The victim was a solicitor and friend of Miss May's; Miss Alice Tanner, she had collapsed while hanging her washing out. Her neighbour Ivy Smith was looking out of her window and saw her hold her stomach before collapsing and called an ambulance. The paramedics could not get in so they phoned the police. Sergeant Taylor had to force the door. When the paramedics gave the possible cause as poisoning I was called.

According to the neighbour, the victim Miss Alice Tanner who kept her self to her self and as far as she was aware never had visitors.

The neighbour, Ivy Smith, spotted Miss Tanner from her window hanging her washing out, she had only hung a few articles on the line before she collapsed and no one was near her at the time.

After searching the property for clues and finding nothing I returned to the station with Constable Forward leaving Sergeant Taylor at the scène. Everything pointed to poisoning, but I couldn't figure out how the killer had carried it out.

I decided to get some of the officers at our station to accompany me to one of our rooms; I hoped someone would come up with a feasible explanation as to how the killer had achieved the murders without being present. The only explanation some one put forward was some sort of poison dart as used in a blow pipe. This was quickly ruled out as the first victim was in her office on the first floor with all the windows shut. I thanked them all for wasting my time and decided nothing could be done till I received the autopsy report.

Miss Tanner worked for a solicitors firm called -Redland & Cottrell, I thought I would go and see if I could find any answers there.

I interviewed Mr Redland who reacted badly to the news of Miss Tanner's death; apparently they had started to meet at his place for dinners and he was hoping for a relationship. He had never been to her home and knew nothing of her home life or friends. He knew of Miss May and said that Mr Cottrell could probably throw some light on a Bill Potter, the man Miss May probably meant as she had discussed the case with him. As Mr Redland was distraught about Miss Tanner I decided to leave him to his grief. Apparently Mr Cottrell was on a week's holiday and would probably be at home tending to his hobby bee keeping.

I decided to go and see Mr Cottrell at his home; his big country house was on the outskirts of town and was very impressive, with a bountiful display of all kinds of flowering plants cloaking his garden. As I got no answer from the front door I decided to go to the rear of the property, I spotted Mr Cottrell at the bottom of his garden with his bee keeping gear on. Luckily for me he was heading back to the house; as he got to me he took off the head gear and I introduced myself, he asked me in and took me to the lounge, once seated I broke the bad news to him, he seemed as upset as Mr Redland and confided he was about to have a relationship with her; She had asked him to spend a few days at her home, I asked if he had ever been to her house he said no and like Mr Redland he new nothing of her private life.

I told him the main reason for my visit was to find out about a Bill Potter an innocent man that Miss May had deliberately got convicted knowing he was innocent. He stared at me with a confused look on his face and asked what that had got to do with Miss Tanner's death.

"That's what I'm here to find out and if he could be involved, Miss May seamed to think he would seek revenge. She too has been murdered this morning." I replied.

"I can't believe it, how did they die? I don't understand. Why?"

"We think they were poisoned but have to wait for the autopsy report before we know for certain"

"I know the man your on about Bill Potter, but he appealed and got acquitted."

"Did he make any threats to anyone involved in the case?"

"No, he just stuck his fingers up to Miss May as he left the court, but said nothing."

"How long ago was this and what was the crime he was accused of?"

"He was accused of grievous bodily harm during a burglary."

"Why was he convicted of the crime? The evidence must have been a bit flimsy if he was found not guilty at the appeal, especially if Miss May knew him to be innocent."

"He had bought a leather brief case from a man in a pub. A police officer recognised it from the description given by the owner, it had a golden eagle embossed on the front and the owner had it inscribed personally so it was the only one."

"Not much to convict someone on, but why would he want to hurt Miss Tanner."

"She deliberately held back evidence proving his innocence, like the fact he was at the pictures five miles away with friends, she just wanted to help Miss May get a conviction, no idea why, perhaps to further her career?"

"Do you have an address for him so I can try and get some answers?"

He told me the last place he knew Bill Potter was living at was 102 Railway Sidings, tower blocks. I thanked him and phoned Sergeant Taylor to meet me there as backup.

We met up and made our way to the top floor and knocked on the door of 102; The door was answered by a nurse who invited us in after checking our identity cards.

Bill Potter still lived here but to our dismay he had been bedridden since he had a fall eight days ago and left him with concussion and broken leg. I was so sure I had found the person responsible but now I was back to square one. Was Bill Potter the man Miss May meant or was there another man out there she had wrongly convicted. I could do nothing more until the autopsy report so I went home early feeling baffled.

The next morning the report was waiting on my desk, I eagerly opened it and learned it was cyanide which kills within seconds but how it was administered escaped me. I got myself a coffee and read the report in full, in the report it was stated that no puncture marks were found on the body and the cyanide according to the coroner was taken orally. With no suspects and no motive I felt I had reached a dead end. While I was giving myself a headache and trying to make headway in the case the phone rang about 9.15am, to my disbelief it was a traffic police officer who had called an ambulance, a man appeared to have had a heart attack at the wheel of his car and the officer had tried to revive him until the paramedics arrived but without any luck, he was told by the paramedics that the man showed signs of poisoning and suggested he phone me as they were the same crew who had attended the last two victims.

I arrived at the scene to find a body lying beside the car covered by a blanket. The car had luckily hit a Royal Mail letterbox saving a mother pushing a baby in a pram further down the path.
The car was a big new Daimler so the man must have been wealthy or perhaps it's a company car for someone high up in that company, I was about to find out.
The traffic policeman introduced himself as Constable Philips and said he had recognised the deceased, a Judge Tomlinson from a court case he had attended. I asked the paramedics if they were sure he had been poisoned, they said they were pretty sure. After looking at the body I told the paramedics to take the body away.
Onlookers claimed that no one was near to the car when it seemed to go out of control. After Constable Philips had checked the car for fowl play it was removed. By the time we left the post office engineers had arrived to re-erect the post box.

Judge Tomlinson I found out, lived within quarter of a mile of the other two victims in a penthouse.

I visited his penthouse with a local locksmith we often used and found it had high security so the only one that would get in was someone he knew, there was a security man that sat in the main hall and according to him judge Tomlinson had not have any visitors today or yesterday. I was starting to get disheartened as the only thing I had to go on was they were all to do with the legal profession. The security man said he would let me in with his pass key so I told the locksmith to go to the station and get paid for his time. The security man accompanied me round the penthouse but I found nothing to indicate who the murderer was. I thanked the security guard and told him someone else from the station would be back for a thorough search.

When I returned to the station, I found out that Judge Tomlinson was the judge that sentenced Bill Potter but Bill Potter was in no fit state to commit any of these crimes. I suddenly had a brain wave what if he wasn't really ill. I sent the police doctor round to examine him; this only confirmed he was as ill as we had been told.

Everything seemed to revolve round that court case so perhaps one of Potters family could be running this vendetta.

Three murders in two days yet no clue to whom or how it was achieved. I decided to trace the son and daughter of Bill Potter to see if they were involved. The daughter had moved away to America but the son was living two miles away in a mobile home which was situated on a site owned by a friend of mine, Ted Tate.

I arrived at the site and went to the office to find out which mobile home he occupied. Ted told me that Potters son Mark was not at home and had not been there for over a week and said Mark Potter was a bit of a loner so knew little about him. He always paid his rent well in advance and would disappear for weeks at a time.
I left my mobile number with Ted so he could let me know when Mark Potter surfaced.

When I returned to the station I went to see the coroner hoping to find out if he had found out anything new. The coroners name was Colin Head but I had never met him before as the last coroner had retired four months earlier. Mr Head was about thirty six and according to gossip not very sociable. I found Mr Head in the morgue preparing to start the post-mortem on judge Tomlinson.

"Hello Mr Head I am Inspector Stewart and I would like to ask you a few questions about the poison victims."

"Can't you see I'm busy? I sent my report don't tell me you can't read?"

I stood and said nothing for a moment trying to control my temper.

"Your report was not 100% clear as to what they had eaten, in fact you never mentioned anything about the contents of their stomachs and perhaps you haven't finished you training yet."

He went red stormed up to me and bellowed in my face.

"Get out and stay out you moron; clear off."

I blew my top and grabbing him bodily I threw him onto one of the slabs.

"Do that again and that's where you will end up, understand? You jumped up cocky little twit." I clenched my fist trying to restrain myself from hitting him. One thing I can't stand is another mans face within inches of mine especially with bad breath. He got off the slab and gingerly made his way to his desk and slumped into his chair.

"Well I'm waiting, three people are dead and it's our job to try and find out who was responsible, I want a report of the stomach contents not just cyanide which gives no clue to how it got there and I would like it on my desk as soon as possible."

He never spoke but wrote on a piece of paper bread, yoghurt, cereal, tea and coffee. "I take it this is a mix of the victim's stomachs? Redo the reports and put the contents of each victim separately when you have finished with judge Tomlinson."

He nodded so I left still feeling a bit shaken; I wondered why he had that big chip on his shoulder, he certainly never had any friends or likely to make any, still who cares. As the victims all died in the first part of the morning it was obvious they had eaten breakfast but Coroner Head had still not been much help, leaving me wondering how to proceed.

I was looking through another case file in the afternoon when my phone rang and to my delight it was Ted Tate informing me that Mark Potter had just turned up. Sergeant Taylor was in the office so I took him along to interview Mark Potter.

We arrived at his mobile home and knocked, hoping to get some answers from him. A tall dark haired man opened the door wearing a smart suit and looked like something out of a gangster movie spats and

all, he even a big scar down his cheek but
has he a gun?

"May we have a few words with you as we
hope you can help with our enquiries? I am
Inspector Stewart and this is Sergeant
Taylor."

"I don't see how but come in providing you
don't take to long as I have to leave here
shortly."

"May I ask what you do for a living?
Apparently you are a bit of a mystery
especially dressed like something out of an
old Al Capone gangster movie? And apart
from making me nervous I definitely need
an answer, just to satisfy my curiosity."

"I am an actor so that's why I don't get to
stay here much, mainly because we tour a
lot so I never see my neighbours, anyway
why does any of my private life involve the
police?"

"Sorry Mr Potter it was seeing you dressed
like that which threw me, the reason we are
here is about when your father was wrongly
convicted of robbery and assault."

"Can't you leave him alone? After all you
lot put him through, he had nothing to do
with that job and you know that so why are
you picking on him now?"

"The barrister, solicitor and the judge involved in that case have been murdered all within the last two days so you can see how it could be some one in your family."

"This better not be a wind up just because I play a gangster, let me see your identity cards or clear off because I don't think it's funny."

We showed our cards and he went pale in the face and sat down.

"My dad is ill and he is a decent man, how dare you try and pin another crime on him haven't you done enough harm to our family?"

"No one is trying to frame your father but we have three murders and they all revolve round that court case. Obviously we had to look for motive and your father came top of the list, don't worry we have ruled your father out as a suspect."

"Ahh! I see, you think I shot those people, well sorry to disappoint you I was with the rest of the cast in Scotland and we only got back here this morning, check if you like."

"I will, not that I disbelieve you but to officially eliminate you from our inquiries."

"That's fair and I am sorry I reacted that way but you did dump a lot on me all at once."

"Good luck with your acting and let me know when your show is in town, I would be very interested in seeing your play that's if it's not fully booked."

"Leave your number and I will get you a couple of tickets and I hope you catch the culprit."

I had forgotten to ask about his sister so I asked Sergeant Taylor to find out her full details then phone the local police in America to check if she had left the country recently. I was running out of suspects, in two days I had eliminated the two main ones leaving me with nothing to go on. I had been so transfixed by Potters court case where I should have been looking at other cases the three victims had been involved in.

After a struggle I managed to convince the court to hand over cases the three victims had been involved in. They soon responded after reminding them that they could be the next victims if I did not solve the case, I sat at my desk and started to wade through them. Halfway through the first case file Constable Forward came into the office and told me the chief inspector wanted to see me urgently.

The chief looked rather annoyed as I entered his office.

"You wanted to see me, is it about the case I'm on?"

"It's indirectly to do with the case, I was informed that you physically assaulted the coroner Colin Head, is that true? If so I want your account of the incident."

After I told the chief exactly what happened he rapped his fingers on his desk a few times then he looked at me and said in a rather gruff voice.

"I am very disappointed in you Inspector Stewart you amaze me, why didn't you deck him, I would have done?"

I stood and looked at the chief; his face still had an angry look on it and I felt confused.

"I thought he would report me I expected nothing else from him, what happens now?"

"He never reported you someone else was passing and witnessed the incident, as to what happens now is you get on and find the murderer and keep away from the morgue."

The rest of the day was spent wading through the case files but they all seemed to say a fair cop and nothing to make some one take a vendetta out on them, in fact the sentences seemed fair and quite light.

It was only the second day and in that short time all I seemed to have done was thrown a smoke screen over the murders.

When I got home, I was so tired I had a hot drink and went straight to bed.

In the morning I sat at the breakfast table and stared at my breakfast which sent a shiver through me, it hit me I could be next and being a bit paranoid I threw it in the bin and grabbed a sandwich from the local shop on the way back to the yard.

As I sat at my desk I could see the reports had been put on my desk from Head the coroner with a note apologising for his behaviour, also if there was anything else he could do to help to let him know.

The last thing I wanted from him was an apology; I just don't like the bloke full stop. Looking through the reports it would appear Miss May had eaten toast, marmalade and had a cup of tea. Miss Tanner had consumed toast, yoghurt and had drunk a coffee. Judge Tomlinson toast and a coffee. The common denominator was toast.

I asked Constable Forward to drive me to all three properties so I could see if all three loafs were the same type. Miss Mays Loaf was a white farmhouse loaf. Miss Tanners was a multigrain loaf and Judge Tomlinson's loaf was a Granary, all three were different makes. What a blow another dead end. Thinking out loud when we got back to the car I said.

"All three were connected by the court and all three lived within quarter of a mile from each other, any suggestions Carol, I mean constable Forward but any suggestions."

"No I am as baffled as you but it might be an idea to see if any other legal people live in this vicinity as they may be in danger."

"Well done constable lets get to the office and make some inquiries."

"I liked it better when you called me Carol Peter, still I can't have everything."

I felt my face glow with embarrassment and she smiled before starting the engine.

Back at the station we started to phone around checking people who live in the same area as the three victims and were working at the court or for solicitors. Constable Forward was really good at research and took less than quarter of an hour to find a clerk who lived in the same area as the three victims.

"Well done constable; See if you can find a phone number for? What's their name?"

"Allan Harper, I think I will phone the court to find out if he is into work today, if not they will have his phone number let's hope he's ok."

She phoned the court and after exclaimed.

"According to the court Mr Harper had turned up for work but was not at his desk; The receptionist said she would send some one to find him and phone us back.

While we waited constable Forward carried on looking for would-be victims and was amazed to find yet another person living within the same area as the other three victims. The phone rang; it was the receptionist returning our call, she said that Mr Harper had been found dead in the men's room.

"We are to late constable, he has been found dead in the men's room better give forensics a call and tell them to meet us at the court."

We arrived at the court where it appeared that Mr Harper had been drying his hands when he died and was alone.

"Better find out if he was married constable or had any relations."

"I will go and check now sir; I suppose we will get the job of informing her, I find it really upsetting informing someone a loved one is dead."

When constable Forward returned she looked puzzled and said.

"That's weird sir all four victims lived alone, perhaps they all belonged to a singles club and it's someone from their club?"

"You frighten me sometimes Constable the way your mind works, how about you make some enquires along them lines, Detective Constable Forward!"

"I would love to be a Detective sir it's been my dream for a long time, it would be great to be a detective."

"Save your dreams for your bed but carry on like you have been and who knows." Once we arrived back at the office Constable Forward wasted no time in getting on the phone to dating agencies.

I went to the men's room and while washing my hands I suddenly remembered, just before the court returned our call Constable Forward claimed she had found another person in that area. Rushing back to her desk I really hoped we were not going to have a fifth victim, she looked shocked that she had forgotten and frantically she rummaged through the papers on her desk and then handed me the address of a person named Annie Draper.

"I really am sorry sir I will phone the court straight away."

"Did you find out what their job is in court? Let's hope we are in time, it seems unreal."

"She is a court stenographer, hang on sir I will phone the court; Hello this is Constable Forward again and I would be grateful if you could find out if Mrs Draper is at work today, Ok thank you that's good news."

"Well what did they say? Is she ok?"

Carol smiled; "That's broken the pattern sir she is on her honeymoon in Jersey."

We both felt relived for the moment but realised she would in danger on her return.

I felt something was wrong with the route I was taking on motives; it was as though I was being misled and the court and half a mile area was all I was given to work on.

"Constable Forward; Do you fancy living your dream as a detective?"

"You mean that sir? What do you want me to do?"

"Find out about the victim's friends to see if there is a connection. Find out everything you can about their lives including Mrs Draper."

"Could take a long time sir so I had better get started, what about my normal duties sir it doesn't leave me much time?"

"Forget everything I will get some one else to cover your work, until this case is closed you are on it with me as I am sure between us we will crack it, well off you go then and keep me informed."

With a big smile on her face off she went.

I stared at the big pile of court case files on my desk then I made myself a coffee and sat at my desk then started to wade through them, hoping there was something in them that could throw some light on these murders. Two hours later, and four more coffees produced a pending migraine and nothing that would give a motivc. As I was only a third of the way through the pile of files I decided to have a break and have a word with Sergeant Taylor.

"Hello Sergeant, if you can spare a few minutes I would like to discuss the poisoning murders with you I just need to clear a few points up."

"Fire away Inspector but I am not sure I can add to the reports."

"Apart from Judge Tomlinson's death you attended all three; did you notice anything in their homes that could connect them, perhaps similar empty food containers all three had?"

"Forensics bagged the pedal bins and took them away so I never got to check.

I thought your mate Head gave you a report on what the victims had eaten sir."

"Firstly that twit head is not my friend and secondly I was more interested in the contents of the bins, mainly because Heads report gave no clues to how the cyanide got into their system, by the way have forensics sent us their report?"

"No I haven't seen a report yet sir and I was only joking about Head being your friend, no one likes him still its early days yet seeing he's only been here for four months."

"I understand he's divorced. How anyone could marry a bad tempered man like that escapes me, maybe he was different before his divorce. I suppose you heard about the incident in the morgue, he does have a violent temper and he has apologised."

"I heard he has given you his hand in friendship sir perhaps you should take it."

"I might get him to open up and find out a bit more about him, not that I'm bothered."

"Don't turn you're back on him sir I never have trusted him as he might try and get his own back on you once you drop your guard. Best just keep away from him. About the report from forensics I will chase them up and bring it to you the minute it turns up."

"Thank you sergeant, I will take your advice and look forward to seeing the report."

With nothing to go on as yet I decided to get stuck into the case files again in the hope I turned something up, all the time I hoped Constable Forward would come rushing in to tell me she had solved the case. By the time I had read the last one it was late in the evening and looking up I noticed that apart from me there was only the cleaner and Joe Tanner who was another inspector left in the office. I locked the case files in my bottom drawer and decided to have a chat with Joe to get his views on the murders.

"Hello Joe looks like your working late too, what are you working on?"

"Nothing as bad as yours, just the robbery at the race track and I think I know who carried it out, it's just a matter of trying to prove it but he's got no alibi and as you know that doesn't convict him."

"Have you got any theories? About these murders as I seem to have drawn a blank."

"Your case is a real stinker Pete, to be honest I have been so involved in my own case I have been oblivious to everything else around me."

"I know the feeling but tell you what Joe how about I treat you to a meal and a drink; we can discuss each others case to clear our heads. What do you say? It's my treat."

"As you're buying let's go for it, I even skipped lunch today and I do need to get my head out of the rut, two heads are better than one so where are we going for the meal?"

"They do good meals at –The Bitch Inn- or I know a good Italian restaurant."

"I like the sound of -The Bitch Inn- makes me tingle at the sound of it so let's go."

"Apart from the waitress and the meal there's not much else to get exited about."

"We said goodnight to Cole the cleaner and checked out with Sid the desk sergeant and then headed for the Inn.

On the way Joe pointed out his suspect talking to another man and started grinning to himself.

"That's the first break I have had in this case thanks to your brilliant idea of going out for a meal it's just clinched my theory so I will treat you."

"You lost me, who was the man he was talking to? Come on I'm waiting."

"That was the manager of the race tracks Willy Trench; Dick Green my suspect said he had never met Willy Trench, I will get a couple of warrant's to search their properties for the 23grand, I guess Willy Trench must have planned it together with Dick Green."

"I guess you will be up bright and early tomorrow to crack your case, well done."

At the meal I told Joe everything which just left him as confused as I was.

The next day at the office Constable Forward was waiting by my desk.

"Morning constable I hope you have got some good news, I found nothing in the files to give a reason as to why someone would be motivated to murder."

"I managed to find where Mrs Draper is staying on her honeymoon, I have talked to her and after explaining the danger she would be in on her return she agreed to extend her honeymoon for an extra two weeks and I said I would phone her as soon as it was safe to return sir."

"Well done, that's a big weight off our minds, have you found anything else out?"

"Have you heard of a club called – The Black Circle – both the lady victims and the Judge belonged to it but as far as I know the clerk didn't?"

"Can't say I have, we will pay it a visit if you have the address, it could be a break."

"I have the address but you can't get in unless you are a member, it's very secret."

"Have you a phone number for the club? I will give them a bell and see what transpires. It all sounds very mysterious."

"Won't do any good sir and I hope you don't mind only I introduced myself as inspector Forward when I phoned them, I was quickly and quite bluntly told to clear off by the man at the club."

"Would you say we have suspicions of drugs at the club Constable?"

"No not really sir. Oh I see what you're getting at and there's one way of getting inside the club."

"You catch on quick, I will contact the drug squad to arrange a surprise search of the premises and then perhaps we might get some answers, do you feel up to it constable?"

"You really mean it sir? I can actually come on the bust with you."

"The bust is only going ahead because of your investigations so be in plain cloths and I will pass you off as an inspector. I want you to interrogate the manager and staff."

"Won't you get into trouble making me out to be an Inspector? Be wonderful sir."
"No one will know; we can get the manager in a room on his or her own out of ear shot." After arranging with the drugs hit squad for 9am the next morning, why 9am, well the club would already have some members there and who knows, who we might find.

The next morning we followed the drug squad to the Black Circle Club hoping for some sort of lead, only to find the club was closed but within seconds the front door was forced and in went the squad. Carol and I headed for the office to locate the manager and thinking this was a real drugs raid the squad were very thorough and not very careful.
Finding the office locked I called for Sergeant Linden the one in charge of the raid and asked for access to the office, he looked really angry and said.
"Who warned them? You want the door open! There how's that?" he shouted as his boot slammed against the lock Smashing the door open and stormed off.
"What have you done sir? Look at the damage, what if they find out this was just to talk to the manager?"

"Are you going to tell them constable?"
Before she could answer Sergeant Linden
came back grinning all over his face.
"Well done inspector Stewart I could kiss
you, on second thoughts I will kiss
Constable Forward."
"Get lost, how about shaking Inspector
Stewarts hand, preferably after you tell us
why you are so happy?"
Sergeant Linden held out a bag of flour.
"I think you should hang on to your contact
look at this."
"So you're going to bake a cake Sergeant,
do you want some pointers from Constable
Forward?"
"Arthur our dog sniffed it out in the bottom
of a waste basket, you can't fool him."
"You have Constable Forward to thank.
Soon I hope to be Inspector Forward."
"I will put in a good word for you, are you
sure I can't give you a kiss as a reward
Carol?"
"I would be grateful if you put in a word for
me but forget the kiss although I'm flattered
you asked. Have you seen the manager?"
"We think he's in his flat is above."
 Sergeant Linden looked at me and said.
"Well Inspector, looks like Forward has

taken over your case so you might as well go home old bean."

I smiled and asked her opinion.

"I think you should concentrate on your task at hand Sergeant Linden and stop making yourself look like a trouble making school boy and as for Inspector Stuart I would be useless without him. I come up with the odd good idea but that's all."

"Sorry I was just having a bit of fun and I will carry out your instructions; our little would be Inspector Forward and find Mr Grainger."

With that he disappeared leaving us to search the office for names or clues to the clubs members. I found an address book which I assumed had the member's names. Careful not to disturb any fingerprints I browsed through the address book and I noticed some pages had been torn out.

"Now we will never know who were on the missing pages sir, what a shame, I wonder who tipped them off. It must have been someone on the force."

"Your forgetting one thing Carol, it's an address book, look a page from D, H, M, T, and W is missing, so what can we conclude from that?"

"Yes you're right sir. Harper, May, Tanner and Tomlinson fit's the victim's surnames, Oh no! The D could be Draper but who is W?" As we stared at the book racking our brains Sergeant Linden entered the office looking straight faced.

"Mr Grainger is upstairs in his flat but he's dead and that's your department inspector." I flicked through the book but no page had been torn out from pages G.

"Thank you Sergeant. Come on constable let's have a look."

As we entered the flat we were amazed at all the expensive items Grainger had acquired.

"There are no signs of a struggle in-fact he looks like he fell asleep in the chair, phone for the forensics and tell Sergeant Linden's men to keep out of here until after forensic team have finished. It looks like he was going to smoke a cigar when he died constable. Can you see why the cigar could have been the cause and why I may have come to that conclusion?"

She stared at the cigar still in his fingers a big expensive cigar and shook her head.

"Look on his coffee table constable."

"His cigar case is open and his own cigars are different to the one in his hand and as far as I can ascertain it was the last thing he did before he died."

"Spot on Constable and if I am not mistaken it was probably laced with cyanide."

"I wonder why he was killed only I would assume he would have been involved with the victims and why kill all these people? Nothing makes sense to me Inspector."

"Have you talked to anyone about this case or about the raid on this club?"

"No, no one in fact you are the only one I have talked to except Sergeant Linden."

"The only one I have discussed the case with is Inspector Roberts but he knew nothing about the raid today and his name is not in the address book I looked."

"We need to check the rest of the names sir just in case one of them can throw a light on the motive behind these murders; at least it's worth a try."

"Have you considered constable that there may be more victims on the missing pages and their surnames start with the same letters as the victims, like Tanner and Tomlinson? I will stay here and wait for the teams to arrive while you get back to the office, check all employees of the court and our department with surnames that may have been on the missing pages and take my car, I will get a lift back to the station with Sergeant Linden."

She looked excited as she took the keys and said.

"Thank you sir, I won't let you down."

The distressing thought that kept running through my mind was that someone from our department could have warned Grainger and then arrived in time to kill him and the killer would have had to know the time of the raid or risk being caught.

When the team arrived I was informed by Simon Watson the Coroner it was his opinion that Grainger died approx 4am, this was another blow because no one could be placed or have an alibi at this time in the morning. I had to admit Constable Forward seemed a likely suspect; she knew all about the case and had not been with me at the time of the murders. It was confirmed by Henry Waters our forensic man that the cigar had been laced with cyanide and when the team removed Grainger, they found another cigar case made to hold three large cigars with one missing. Why would he be up at 4am to smoke a cigar? His bed had been slept in and he was wearing his pyjamas and dressing gown. I decided the only explanation was someone had left the cigars then phoned him around 4am to warn him of the raid and let him know of the cigar case they had left him.

I could only hope the killer had slipped up and left his number but checking the phone found the caller had withheld their number.

After Linden dropped me off at the station I contacted the phone company; they informed me a call to the club had been made at 3.48am from believe it or not the police station and in fact my extension. Someone was taking the rise out of me and the first person I needed to question was sergeant Kemp the desk sergeant. He claimed there were only he and the cleaner there but the cleaner had left by 10.30pm. Someone is running circles round me but sooner or later they will make a mistake.

The only other way into the station is at the back of the building leading into the car park, the door had been forced but I just stared at the damage knowing something was wrong, then it hit me the damage had been caused by a crowbar but levered from the inside and It would appear someone was breaking out not in. This could be the first break for me as there is a CCT camera pointed at the back door and another covering the car park.

Terry Carter is in charge of the CCT equipment and I found him in the mess room and was only to glad to help. After spinning through the footage we found no one had made an exit through that door but we did see the door open slightly when it was jemmied at 3.40am.

"Thank you Terry but could anyone have tampered with this equipment?"

"No only the chief and I have a key to this room and anyway I would have picked it up just by looking at the footage, the display shows the time right to the second."

I thanked him again and found it very disheartening.

I needed to talk over the events with someone outside the force as I could no longer trust anyone in the police station. My old school friend Mick was good at working out problems and trustworthy as they come so I gave him a call in anticipation he may help.

Owing to a heart problem Mick had retired from work early so was at home most of the time. He said he would be glad to help and told me to pop round. After catching up on each others news I started to tell him in confidence what had happened so far and the dead ends I had come up against. First thing he did was open a map and mark the places of the incidents.

"Tell me Pete did you check the windows on the ground floor for tampering?"

"I did that's what is so worrying because someone working there must have left the catch off the window at the side of the building before they left work, that's not covered by CCT then they returned later, climbed in jemmied the rear door and phoned the club and left the same way; then secured the window when they returned to work as normal the next morning. The window is never used but had been recently opened going by the scuff marks in the dust and dirt scuffs on the windowsill"

Mick replied. "As the victims all died by cyanide it would be safe to assume the same person was responsible for the death of Mr Grainger. Tell you what puzzles me is you said all the doors in the club were locked, secondly why leave a bag of flour containing drugs knowing the dog would find them and why not take the address book instead of leaving it to be found?"

"That's what's been puzzling me to, If the club was running drugs then they would have tried to hide the fact as you say; Mr

Grainger had his keys in his jacket pocket so who would have a second set?"

Mick got up deep in thought and disappeared into the kitchen; he returned with two coffees and said.

"Perhaps it was a girlfriend or his boss."

"Sounds feasible and your best point Mick, is why did they remove odd pages from the address book instead of taking the whole thing; unless I'm being given a false trail?"

"Exactly what I was thinking and to be quite honest can you be sure the victims were members of the club, don't you think it strange no one was hanging around wondering why the club hadn't opened."

He was right and all those things had gone through my mind at the time but the way it had been planned blinded me to act on the obvious.

"I have the horrible feeling that what you're trying to tell me is Grainger and the club were used, just to throw me off the track and confuse me."

"If you want my advice Pete I would forget about Grainger and the club for now and find out where your Constable Forward got her information about the club and then I think you may be a bit nearer to catching the killer, to be honest I would lay a trap for your Constable."

"I would hate to think she is involved but I will take your advice on board."

"Your trouble is you haven't taken time to relax and given your brain chance to focus. The killer has given you to much information over a short period of time so no arguments just put your feet up for a couple of hours while I put on some of the music on we like and I will make some cheese on toast. Just relax and we can talk over old times."

He was right I felt the thick headache gradually disperse as we talked and laughed about our past escapades giving me a clearer view of the case from a new angle. "Tell you what Pete how about we make my study into your temporary office then we can discuss any further developments together. Be like old times, that's if you think it would help?"

"I have really enjoyed this morning I feel great Mick, perhaps I could pop in after work each day and we can work on the case together. Well I had better make a move and thank you for everything Mick and I will see you tomorrow evening."

"Can you make it before 7pm on Tuesday's and Friday's? As my girlfriend comes round at that time and I stay at her place Saturday nights."

I thanked him again and left.

When I returned to the station I asked Sergeant Kemp on the front desk if he had seen Constable Forward; he said she hadn't as yet turned up for work. Something was wrong as it was now 2.45pm and she had not clocked in. I found Sergeant Taylor and asked him to accompany me to her house.

After getting no answer when we phoned we left and arrived at her semidetached house. She appeared to be out; I looked through the garage window and noticed her car was still there with her in the driver's seat.

"Sergeant we need to get in the garage as she is sitting in her car slumped forward."

"The garage door is unlocked sir."

The car windows were all open and the ignition was switched on.

"She is still alive sir but there is a big bump on the back of her head."

"Looks like someone tried to gas her as the ignition is on. There is still plenty of fuel left so I wonder why the engine stopped?"

I looked round the back of the car.

"She had backed onto an old rolled up carpet when she put the car away Jack and the end of the exhaust is against it which chocked the engine, lucky girl."

Sergeant Jack Taylor phoned for an ambulance, after securing Constable Forward in an upright position in the car I searched for any clues, she appeared to be breathing ok so hopefully the bang on the head hadn't caused any serious damage. I told Sergeant Taylor to go in the ambulance with her to the hospital and stay there in case a further attempt was made on her life. Perhaps she had asked one too many questions, only she could say.

I found her handbag at the side of her bed with the contents tipped out along with all the drawers in the house. I guessed what they were after was Constable Forwards note book. If I had been looking for it I would have tried her uniform first which she kept out of sight in a suitcase under the stairs and the reason was she was scared all her friends and neighbours would give her a wide berth, she told all of them she worked for a solicitor as a secretary. She took the suitcase to work and got changed as her friends would exclude her from their lives if they knew she was a police officer.

There under the stairs was the case and her uniform and bingo the note book.

I headed for my office but then thought better of it; instead I thought I would go to my friend Mick just to be on the safe side. I phoned him to say I was on my way but he told me to keep away as he noticed his house was being watched. How could someone have known I had been to Mick's, I know I was not followed? Feeling a bit paranoid I took my jacket off and searched it for a tracker and there in the lining was the offending article. I drove to a continental carrier service and tossed it in one of their containers leaving for Holland; let's see what they make of that.

I went to the local library to study the note book in private and found nothing that could incriminate anyone as far as I could ascertain. The note book I hid under the carpet in the boot of my car and headed for the hospital.

Constable Forward was awake and sitting up a good sign I thought except she had amnesia. She could not remember anything after leaving the Black Circle Club. I had a word with the sister in charge and she agreed to let us borrow a nurse's uniform for constable Forward so we could sneak her out the back way. Sergeant Taylor stayed behind guarding the empty room to make out she was still there.

A lady friend I knew ran a small clothes shop so I took her there. Gracie Day was only too pleased to help; she said she would put her up for a few days providing I took her out for an evening meal, once my friend Carol was better. I reluctantly agreed or so I pretended but in reality I was over the moon at the idea of a date with Grace.

As I returned to the station I was met by Sergeant Linden of the drugs squad. "Peter that bag of flour we found, it only had just enough drugs in the top of it for our dog to home in on, it looks like someone is playing with us so be wary and don't take anything for granted, it looks to me like a red herring."

"Did you tell anyone apart from you men about the raid, I take it you trust them all?"

"With my life, there is not one of my team that is not 100% committed and loyal."

"That just leaves Constable Forward and I just hope I'm wrong about her."

"She would be my best bet because none of my men knew till that morning; the killer would have had to known the night before. Who told her there were drugs at that club?" I had to keep up the pretence and replied. "An anonymous phone call I believe, she is in the hospital with a slight concussion and amnesia." He looked puzzled and asked. "How did that happen? I will have to go and see her and ask her a few questions." "Sorry to say she is incoherent and not allowed any visitors but as soon as she is they will phone me, then I will let you know straight away"

He looked a bit put out then nodded.

"I would be grateful if you could, I hope she soon recovers I might get some answers."

It would appear the killer had been a bit to clever and careless in disposing of Constable Forward. All I could hope for was that her memory would return before the killer struck again.

I returned to her home and called on all her nearby neighbours hoping I could get a description of the caller. Most of the neighbours were out except a Miss Jessup across the road; aged 76 but still in command of all her faculties, she claimed the only caller Carol had was the milkman. She did however have her breakfast in her conservatory at the rear and she only glanced out the front window once. At least I could add one caller to my investigation.

I could ask the milkman if he noticed any other callers. The other neighbours I talked to had claimed the only people they had noticed that called at Miss Forward's house were the police being Sergeant Taylor and myself.

I decided to call at (Early Bird Dairies) the local dairy to interview the milkman. The Manager Mr Curd was a bit alarmed at the thought of the police wanting to talk to one of his employees.

"All my employees are long serving and very honest; what's this all about?"

"Don't worry Mr Curd I just want to talk to the milkman who delivers to 27 Hopper Pickers drive. He may have noticed something this morning that could help me in my investigations."

He took me to his office and opened his large old book that had seen better days.

"Sally Knight is the only one that delivers to Hopper Pickers drive and only to 3-18-23 and 29."

"I was told that a milkman had called to 27 not a woman, could one of your other staff have 27 on their round?"

"No definitely not, no-one would ever pilfer some one else's patch."

Nothing seemed straight forward in this case.

"Where is the next nearest dairy? Trust me to pick the wrong dairy; Sorry about that."

"The nearest other dairy is (Daisy Chain Dairy's) 15miles away; it would not be worth their trouble to come all this way and not cost effective. Want their Number?"

"Yes please that will save me a lot of time; thank you for all your help."

I phoned and as Mr Curd had predicted they only call on their local area. He never gave his name but he did suggest I checked the local dairy farms as they sometimes deliver their own milk straight from their farm. The only one he knew of was (Great Udders Farm). I thought he was joking about the name, but yes he was right, so off I set.

After wading through mud, cows! And cow's muck I tracked the farmer down in one of the outbuildings; he said he had stopped delivering his milk, now he sold the milk from the farm house. Back to square one again. Great!!

The only way forward was to go back to Miss Jessup and ask some more questions.

She seemed pleased I had come back and apologised for still being in her dressing gown. The reason she had not got dressed was she never had visitors; she insisted I stayed for a cup of tea and biscuits; I didn't need much persuading as my tongue was hanging out. She brought in the tea tray then disappeared for ten minutes before returning. Dressed, and wearing a big smile.

"Inspector Stewart would you mind bringing the tray out to the conservatory? It's much nicer and brighter out there."

"Ok Miss Jessup I just need clarification about the man you saw at Miss Forward's house this morning."

I just remembered in time not to let on Carol is a Constable as she had kept the fact she was in the force a secret from her friends and neighbours. I asked her to describe the man she saw and why she thought he was a milkman and after a pause she said.

"I only saw the back of him but he had a white overall jacket on and he had a milk carrier in his hand containing two bottles of milk."

"What did his milk float look like and did it have a name or logo on the side?"

"I never saw a vehicle but I don't always see Sally's float, some times she leaves it outside her house at number two, she is lovely and knocks to see if I'm ok."

"You mean Sally Knight from early Bird Dairies?"

"Yes. Fancy you knowing her are you courting her Inspector?"

"Alas no I have haven't met her; I went to the dairy and found out she delivered in this drive. What a stroke of luck that she lives in the drive, do you know when she's home?"

"You might just catch her as she puts in a couple of hours at the charity shop."

I quickly drank my tea, thanked Miss Jessup and I made my way to number two.

A very healthy cheerful lady answered the door.

"Hello Miss Knight, I am Inspector Stuart and I would like to ask you a few questions if I may." She looked concerned and after checking my identity card invited me in.

"Don't worry Miss it's nothing concerning you but I would like to know if you noticed anything strange this morning, perhaps a man posing to be a milkman?"

"You had me worried for the moment I thought something had happened to one of my customers and to answer your question no I don't remember seeing a stranger this morning but I deliver to number 29 and they phoned me up and told me someone had walked off with their milk carrier containing the two pints of milk I left this morning."

"What time did you leave the milk? it may help us pinpoint the time of the incident?"

"You're not telling me an inspector has been assigned because of to pints of milk?"

"No someone posing as a milkman tried to kill Miss Forward this morning and it would appear he used the stolen carrier to add to his disguise, what time did you call and leave the milk at number 29 as near as possible please."

"How dreadful I hope she's ok; I did notice a milk carrier the same as 29's, on the door step at Miss Forward's house after my round and I felt a bit put out that she hadn't asked me to deliver her milk and that was about 8.30am. What you're telling me is that the carrier was stolen from number 29."

"Yes but I will be picking it up and the milk for forensic testing, just in case the perpetrator slipped up and left fingerprints or DNA then it will be returned. Not sure if the milk will still be ok but they can claim."

After picking up the carrier I decided to find a pay phone and give Gracie Day a bell just to see how Constable Forward was getting on. Gracie informed me that apart from recurring blurred vision and migraine she was fine. She said she got on well with Carol and the pain killers she had bought from the chemist were doing the trick. Gracie made sure Carol stayed out of sight but as the pain killers made Carol sleep most of the time it wasn't a problem.

I contacted Sergeant Taylor to find out if anyone had tried to get into constable Forwards room at the hospital. Apart from a cleaner whom he turned away no one had been near. Sergeant Linden had phoned the hospital to enquire as to her situation but he was told that because of her injuries she could not have any visitors.

When I arrived at the station I dropped the milk carrier off at the forensics lab and asked why they had not sent me any reports of their findings so far. They seemed puzzled and claimed they had left it on my desk, the same day Sergeant Taylor had torn them off a strip for dragging their heels. That's worrying, the though of someone with free access to come and go as they please in the station, and it makes the police station the most unsafe place to be until this case is solved. After insisting I have an up to date report by the end of the day I headed back to Early Bird Dairies.

As all victims had been poisoned in the first part of the morning and as the person posed as a milkman at Forwards address, I had to check if the victims had milk delivered. It was possible that as the victims all lived in the same area that they may have had the same milkman.

Mr Curd was in his office eating fish and chips when I arrived and his mug of tea must have held a pint, I think he must have lived on that sort of food as his stomach oozed over his belt. He seemed annoyed to see me again and this made me instantly suspicious of him.

"Hello Mr Curd, Sorry to interrupt your lunch but I need some information from you, after your lunch would be ok."

He sat there stuffing his face and swilling it down with his tea.

"Take your time there's no hurry and don't give yourself indigestion."

He went red in the face as if he was going to blow his top. To save him having a heart attack I waited outside his office, the other reason? Watching him gorge himself made me feel sick. He finally appeared at his office door belching and stinking of vinegar as he wiped tomato sauce off his chin.

"What do you want now? I haven't done anything."

His attitude and mannerism sent alarm bells ringing so I played a blinder.

"The game is up Mr Curd I know everything so if you waist one more minute of my time I will throw the book at you, I will go easy on you if you come clean."

He turned and went back in his office and I followed. A locker looking worst for wear stood in the corner of his office and after fumbling with his keys, his shaking hands opened the locker to reveal two big boxes. Mr Curd placed both on his desk looking terrified, wondering what my reaction would be to the contents.

One contained pouches of tobacco, filter tips and papers. The other contained packets of cigarettes.

"I only sell it to my staff as a favour and only charge the same as I paid, that's all."

"Do you smoke Mr Curd? Because if you do and continue with you're eating habits, it's a safe bet your staff will be attending your funeral before long."

"What happens now? Are you going to confiscate the lot? I'm ruined."

"Chuck that lot back in the locker, perhaps I can look at the ledger of your customers, |I just need to see who delivers to a certain area."

"Of course wait a minute, there the desk is clear. What about the smokes."

"I am on a murder investigation and all I am interested in is the ledger. Anyway you're not making money on it and it's just a perk for your staff so keep it in house. Can we get on with the ledger because there is a killer out there? I'm trying to catch."

A Mr Sidney Ware delivered to the first three victims and Mr Arthur Simms delivered to the clerk Allan Harper. They all had milk delivered but not the same milkman.

"Can you check and tell me if the two milkmen in question did their own rounds on those dates? And did you deliver to the Black Circle Club?"

"Yes they were on their own rounds and no, the Black Circle Club is not one of our customers, in fact it hasn't been a club for about four years. A man called Mark Grainger looks after the place for Mr Trent the owner who lives abroad."

"Mr Grainger no longer looks after Mr Trent's property as we found him dead this morning. Do you know of any scams going on there?"

"He seemed a very fit chap, although he liked his cigars and before you ask he always came here and bought his butter milk and bread that's how I know."

"You never answered my question, was Mr Grainger up to anything at the club?"

"I think he went to auctions because he tried to sell me a watch he had bought at an auction but nothing dodgy that I know of. As for a heart attack, that would have been the last thing he would die of you can ask the gym he went to."

"Would that be the keep fit place next to - The Vicars Retreat- pub?"

"That's the one, he told me he went there every Tuesday and Thursday."

"Thanks for that but before I go, can you write the names and addresses of the two milkmen, I just want to see if they noticed anything strange on the days in question?"

He scribbled the names and addresses on a piece of paper and handed it to me.

"Am I in trouble with the law about anything, Inspector?"

"Not that I know of Mr Curd and thank you for all your help, I'm very grateful."

By this time I was getting a bit weary, I headed home to think things over before my mind was clouded by more information. I made a hot malt drink and watched a film before falling asleep in front of the television. I was woken up by some loud music on the television about half one in the morning and a painful stiff neck. After taking some pain killers I felt confused, I couldn't get this milkman theory out of my head. All the victims died early part of the morning and unless their milkman was like my old one we called the midnight milkman, mainly because he turned up at 5.30pm with milk warm enough to make my malt drink with, they would have called at the victims homes early before they died. The only problem was two different milkmen were involved. Mr Head the coroner could not see anything in their stomachs to explain how the Cyanide was administered. The person that tipped Constable Forward off about the club must be the killer but why bother risking attaching Grainger's murder with the others? Why not bump him off in a different way, unless the killer is so conceited and right under my nose.

I think everyone is guilty of over looking things that are staring them in the face and that is what I must be doing. I must get some sleep and in the morning I will take a look at the case from a completely different angle. I was out like a light as soon as my head hit the pillow.

The good news was my stiff neck had gone when I woke up but the frustration was still giving me a thick head.

I was still paranoid about eating breakfast so after my cup of tea I called at the bakers on the way to work and I had them make me a couple of sandwiches. I got myself a drink from the machine at the station then sat at my desk eating my sandwiches and noticed the forensic report by its absence. When I phoned down to them I was told it had been put on my desk yesterday afternoon. I never returned to the office yesterday as I went straight home and missed my chance to catch the culprit. I told them I would pick it up myself as soon as they had redone it.

The gym was my next port of call, anything to try and get a lead. Andy Trip the manager of the gym claimed that the late Mr Grainger was a very private man and kept himself to himself. I thanked him and left but as I got to my car Mr Trip ran up to me with a piece of paper.

"Hang on Inspector this man normally turned up with him and I was under the impression they were old friends, you should get all the info you need from him."

"Thank you, very much appreciated, you have saved me a lot of time."

I shook his hand and headed for the address on the paper. Samson-Towers.

It was a luxury block of apartments so this Mr Tony Sparrow was well off or up to his ears in debt. Apartment 36 was on the top floor and the lift was out of action. When I had climbed the flights of stairs to the fourth floor I had to sit on the top stair to get my breath back. Normally I am fairly fit but the stress and missing meals, on top of the broken sleep was taking its toll. The door bell was loud and as I never got an answer he must have been out. As I started to walk away the next apartment front door opened; a well spoken lady who must have been well past retirement age and holding a cat exclaimed.

"He's in 24 with that tart; tell him his door bell is too loud as I keep being woken up and it upsets my Sooty."

"Thank you madam I will convey your message and thank you for the info."

I headed back down the stairs and found number 24 then rang the bell.

Just a gentle ding dong rang out, a man with thick ginger hair and wearing a track suit stood in the doorway looking annoyed.

"If you're selling you can clear off. What do you want?"

"I understand you were a friend of Mr Grainger and I would like to ask you a few questions about him, as he seemed to be a bit of a mystery."

"What do you mean were his friend? I still am and if you want to know anything about him I suggest you ask him yourself. Now clear off."

"Being his best friend, I thought you would be only too pleased to help me catch his killer and by the way I am Inspector Stewart and I would like some answers."

He stood there and went a ghostly white, not saying a word but just beckoned me in. An attractive middle aged woman with long jet black shiny hair was wearing a tea shirt and shorts and peddling away on a keep fit cycle.

"Hello who are you? I'm Tina Trent."

Tony Harrow appeared in the room looking scared and staring at the floor, he was deep in thought.

"What's up Tony, what's wrong sweetheart, who are you what have you said to him?"

"I am Inspector Stewart, Mark Granger has been murdered and I need Mr Harrow to help me in my investigation, would you both sit on the settee as time is of the essence."

"How did Mark die inspector? I have known him for over forty years, I can't believe it."

"Someone laced a cigar with cyanide but it was not one he normally smoked, the cigar was a large expensive one, any idea of anyone he new that smoked that type?"

"He did have a visitor who smoked big cigars but I never met him, I saw the butt of one in his ashtray and remarked he must have won the pools."

"Can you remember any little remark he made about his visitor? Please think it's very important, Mr Grainger is the fifth person the murderer has killed and you two may be in danger especially if you know anything that may lead to their arrest."

"Mark said it was an old friend he used to work with and he could be on a good earner with him."

"What type of work was that and can you remember the name of the firm they worked at?"

"-Turnaround pharmaceuticals- Mark was brilliant at his job but he got the sack for making drugs on the quite and selling them, the firm kept it quite and did not report it to the law. Trouble was, instead of being grateful he, hang on! If I knew he was breaking the law and never reported it, does that make me an accomplice?"

"This conversation is between us and off the record; if you were not directly involved in his dealings then we never had this conversation, now tell me everything."

"Mark has a lockup he bought on the - Greenstones industrial Estate- next to the railway track, I'm not sure but one day I was at his place when a parcel was delivered, it contained test tubes so I assumed he still dabbled. Perhaps that's what he did in the lockup, I did ask if I could see the lockup but he said it was private. I thought we were close but after that I felt he was up to no good."

"You have been more of a help than you know and for your own safety neither of you mention my visit to anyone. Miss Trent, do you have anything to add before I leave?"

"Mark used to visit us but I'm sure he said he had a friend in the police force, yes he did, Tony, do you remember you told him to keep his nose clean and he said his friend in the force would see him alright because he was owned a big favour."

"Wait a minute, Mark said his friend was smoking one of those big cigars and remarked they must pay well in the force, If the killer is in the force we could be next."

"Don't worry but just in case pack some stuff and if you have someone to put you up I will drive you there, don't worry I don't smoke cigars."

They looked panicky and Miss Trent told me her parents owned a farm 17 miles away and wanted to call them, I stopped her in case the phone was tapped.

My mobile had gone flat earlier that day so I had decided to leave it like that till I got back to the station.

The killer seems to have access to tracking facilities and I'm fed up with them being one step ahead. I dropped the two of them off at her parent's farm.

Next stop was the address given to me by Mr Curd for the milkman that delivered to the first three deceased. Mr Ted Gunter lived in a small cottage at the bottom of -Creeping Ivy Lane- on the edge of town. I could see he liked gardening; in fact he could open it to the public as it was that colourful. I spotted him pruning a lovely pink rose bush and introduced myself. I asked if he had noticed anything out of the ordinary on that fateful day, he could only remember one thing that made him suspicious. When he delivered to Miss May a car was parked further down the road and the only reason he remembered the car was he used to own it, a blue Sunbeam Alpine which is rarely seen on the roads these days. That was fair enough he said but when he delivered to Miss Tanner the same car had parked at the end of that road as if it had followed him. He thought he was being sized up to be robbed; he got his wheel brace and started towards the car which smartly did a u-turn and drove off.

"Why didn't you come forward with this information earlier?"

"I never connected someone trying to rob me with the murders; as I drove out the street I noticed the same car re-enter the road from the other end but I never saw it again after that."

"Will Mr Simon Heard be at home at this time? I believe he delivered to Judge Tomlinson's house the following day only I need to ask him some questions?"

"You will find him in the Vicars Retreat. He more or less lives in there, if he's not to drunk you may get some sense out of him."

After praising Mr Gunter on his garden I headed back to town and the Vicars Retreat.

I found Mr Heard sitting alone with a pint of bitter in his hand and a glass of whisky on the table.

"Hello Mr Heard I am inspector Stewart and I would like to have a word with you.

"I walked here inspector so I won't be driving home, I don't drink and drive."

"I bet you're over the limit when you drive your float in the morning; still I'm not interested in that unless you kill someone. I won't to know if you noticed anything strange the day Judge Tomlinson died when you delivered his milk."

"No not that I recall but I thought I saw Ted up the road in his sports car."

"You mean his Blue Sunbeam Alpine which was classed as a sports car in its time."

"How do you know Ted had that car? Anyway it wasn't him because I remembered he sold it about seven years ago to some surgeon. Ted was a bit reluctant as he doesn't smoke and the bloke who wanted to buy it smoked cigars."

"So why did he sell it to him if he thought the man would ruin the interior?"

"The man swore he never smoked in the car and offered him an extra £200."

"Did you get a look at the man or can remember anything else?"

"I never met him, Ted never liked him but the £200 extra swayed him."

I know I shouldn't have but I bought him another pint and left to return to Mr Gunter.

As I neared the entrance to the lane I noticed the Blue Sunbeam Alpine zooming up about five hundred yards behind me. As it got closer it suddenly slapped on its brakes and did a broadside, spinning round it shot off in the opposite direction.

He must have been on his way to silence Mr Gunter and then recognised my car.

Mr Gunter was just getting in his car when I arrived; he told me he was on his way to the station to see me. He took me indoors and handed me some papers. The documents were copies of the sale of his Sunbeam Alpine and he pointed to the buyer's name, Mr M Grainger. He had told Mr Gunter he was buying it for his friend Colin, who had always dreamed of owning one, especially in showroom condition like mine."

"I talked to your college Mr Heard, you gave him the impression you never liked This Mr Grainger, was there any reason for this?"

"Mr Grainger was ok; it was the one he was buying it for I didn't like. He phoned his friend Colin to convince me that he would not smoke in the car. His friend said he only smoked at home but it was his attitude, the jumped up cocky little twit."

"What did you just call him? I called someone else that and his name was Colin."

"Hang on inspector I have a message on my mobile, I will have to stop putting it on silent. It's just one of my friends asking me to a barbeque, I will just reply to them."

After he had sent the text, he suggested we had a cup of tea and see if he could remember anything else about Mr Grainger and his friend. I suddenly felt a forbidding feeling just like I had when I was a kid walking past a dark room, I put it down to finding out Colin Head may be the killer. "I think I can hear a car coming down the lane, probably the postman; anyway can you get my post while I do the tea, if you don't mind?"

I walked out the front door and to my horror the Blue Sunbeam Alpine turned into the drive. Colin Head got out and walked towards me brandishing a revolver. "You finally worked it all out; still you won't be telling anyone you cocky twit." He said as he grinned and waved the gun at me, he walked up to within ten foot of me and raised his gun. I heard a loud gun shot and I felt a plash of wet hit me in the face, I put my hands to my face, I was covered in blood. They say all your life flashes before your eyes when you die but I saw nothing, my mind went blank and a morbid feeling of dread engulfed me. I felt no pain just my stomach screwed up in knots. I looked down expecting the ground to come zooming towards me but instead Colin Head lay a few feet away in a pool of blood and a big hole in his chest.

It was his blood all over me. As I stared at him I felt as if someone had poured ice cold water in the top of my head, it seem to trickle down my arteries filling my whole body.

"Are you ok Inspector?"

I turned to see Mr Gunter holding a 12 bore shotgun with both barrels still smoking.

"I keep it for protection but never thought I would use it to save an inspectors life; it's a good job I heard the sound of my old car, I would recognise it anywhere."

A tap opened in my toes and the ice water trickled away as my senses returned back to reality. He showed me his licence for the shotgun before putting it on the hall table but still feeling a bit shaken I sat down.

"Thank you for saving my life and can I use your land line? My mobile hasn't got a very good signal, perhaps you know a company that has a better coverage?"

He wrote his supplier on a piece of paper so I took it and then phoned the station. I told Sergeant Kemp on reception what had happened and he dispatched a crew straight away.

"Would you mind if I get cleaned up a bit, at least get this blood off my face?"

"Go ahead Inspector feel free; I will put a blanket over the dead man."

"No! Don't go anywhere near him till the forensic team have finished with body and taken their pictures. I can do with that cup of tea, I still feel a bit shaken even thought it was not my blood, I thought I was going to die and thanks again."

I washed my face and hands but my head was still in a spin and my hands were still shaking as I cupped them round my mug of tea.

Sergeant Taylor was on the scene first and was concerned about me and suggested I should have counselling; the thought of someone messing with my brain made me cringe, all I wanted was to be left alone.

"Come on Peter let me get you back to the station, nothing else you can do here, I think its best you leave the scene as soon as possible as I can see you're still shaken."

"Your right Sergeant, I would like to get out of these blood stained clothes and have a nice long hot shower, can someone else take my car back? I can go with you."

"Be glad to and well done on solving the case, we can all sleep better tonight."

Sergeant Taylor shook Mr Gunter's hand and thanked him. When the rest of the team arrived Sergeant Taylor drove me to my house.

I asked him to wait so he could drive me back to the station afterwards, which he tried to talk me out of.
He made himself a cup of coffee and turned the television on to watch the sport.
After my shower I got dressed and sat opposite him to relax for five minutes before returning to the station.
"You've cut your hand Sergeant, how did you do that? Unless its Heads blood, perhaps when you inspected the body?"
"I never went near the body and I haven't been near enough to you so I don't know."
That old morbid feeling started to raise its ugly head again and things started to flash through my head as the shock started to wear off.
"You shook hands with Gunter and the blood is on the inside of your right wrist, which would match with shaking his hand."
"Well that's another mystery solved, I will go and wash it off then we can get going."
"By the way Sergeant, who did you leave guarding Constable Forward's Hospital Room?"

"No one I told the hospital staff she had been moved to a nursing home at the coast." I had a gut feeling something is wrong, how did Gunter get blood on his jacket sleeve? He never went near the body, unless he went to Heads body while I was having a wash.

"I remembered when Head raised his gun he looked to the side and smiled, why smile at a man pointing a twelve bore shotgun at you, unless he thought it was to kill me?"

"Wait sir, before we jump to conclusions let me phone forensics, if they are still there."

He phoned them and asked a few questions.

"Your right, they said the blood on Heads chest has a smear across it as if his wallet was removed."

"Tell them to take Gunter into custody and I remember something else that never registered at the time, tell them to pick up the ashtray in the bathroom, there is a cigar butt in it. All that talk about not smoking I bet he is the cigar smoker."

"You could be right sir but what is the motive behind the murders?"

"Can you drive me to Greenstones Industrial Estate, Grainger has a Lockup there."

"Sounds promising Sir, are you nearly ready to leave?"

"Yes, I think we will find out quite a lot once we get in there we can interview Gunter when we get back to the station, so let's get going."

We arrived at the industrial estate but Sergeant Taylor didn't wait to see if the estate manager had a key, he grabbed a crowbar out of his boot and broke off the padlock. Inside looked like a laboratory, it looked like Tony Harrow was right about Mark Grainger.

"Get our best Forensic person here as quick as you can Sergeant, this is well above our heads, see if Mary Emery is available as she is about the only one that stands a chance of knowing what he was up to."

She was on sight within twenty minutes and spent about fifteen minutes looking at everything without saying a word. Sergeant Taylor looked at me and shrugged his shoulders. She finally picked up a small capsule and placed it in my hand. "I have got to do some tests but I am pretty sure that this capsule is how your killer did it and that would take about 1-2hrs to dissolve in the stomach, that's why the killer was no where around when they died."

"They are not much bigger than mustard seeds, would one be enough?"

"I would imagine more than one would have been used but I haven't a clue how."

"How could he make something so intricate, it's amazing?"

"Shame he didn't use his genius for good. I will stay here and analyse his equipment, it would be too dangerous to remove anything back to my laboratory at present."

"Get two more officers to guard the door Sergeant, I will get back and interview Mr Gunter, Join me once they have arrived."

Mary was like a kid with a new toy, eyes wide open with an exited look on her face.

"I think we will have to drag her out from here, don't you agree Sergeant?"

"I think your right there sir, see you later."

Back at the station Mr Gunter was being held in the interview room but first I wanted to finally see the forensic report. I assumed it was Colin Head that kept it from me. In the report it clearly stated that in the contents taken from the 1st four victims pedal bins they found an empty promotional pack of yogurt along with an empty sachet of seeds to mix with it. The label boasted great alertness and energy, they must have been left by Gunter with the milk but why kill all those people? I was about to find out at least that's what I was hoping. With this new information I headed for Gunter.

The two arresting officers were with him. I got one of the officers outside and asked if they had found the wallet Gunter had removed from Head but no such luck. "Is there anyone still at the property Constable? If so find that wallet and send more men if you need to as because it's very important."

I entered the interview room and looked at Gunter grinning all over his face.

"I saved your life so what's all this about? Talk about gratitude."

"I'm hoping your going to tell me, for a start where is Heads wallet."

"I don't know I never took it, I never went near the body and you know that."

"You had chance while I was washing the blood off my face remember."

"I swear to you I never left the cottage, why do you think it was me, why! tell me?"

"Let me see your right hand sleeve, Head smiled at you just before you shot him."

"He was at the dairy the day before those people died, he must have recognised me."

"You seemed calm about the shooting; in fact you seemed cold and unaffected."

"I was in the war and some of my comrades died because someone hesitated. When I saw the car and then the gun instinct cut in, we would both be dead now if I hadn't."

"Let me have a look at your mobile, the text you sent while I was there, may have been to bring him there to silence him and convince me he was the murderer."

"Your right look at my sleeve, there is blood on it but there can't be I was to far away from the body you have to believe me."

He sounded really convincing and if he was telling the truth the only other way the blood could have got on his sleeve was when he shook hands with Sergeant Taylor. My heart jumped in my mouth as Taylor was alone with Mary Emery at the lockup.

"Constable, quickly find out if two officers have been sent to Greenstones Industrial Estate at Sergeant Taylor's request and get Sergeant Linden, tell him it's urgent."

Sergeant Linden seemed the only one I could trust.

"Wait constable forget Linden just get two constables with fire arms and accompany me but say nothing to anyone else."

He came back with two young burly armed constables. I left one to guard Gunter with the other constable and took the second constable and the other armed officer with me.

When we arrived at the lock up no one was at the door so quietly the armed officer followed me in. Sergeant Taylor had his back to us searching through a drawer and Mary Eaton was lying on the floor, either dead or unconscious. I had told the armed officer on the way in not to take any chances. The officer cocked his revolver and hearing the sound Taylor quickly reached into his pocket as he spun round. Without hesitation the officer fired sending Taylor reeling against the filing cabinet before slumping to the floor. "Taylor was reaching for a gun sir but don't worry I only shot him in the shoulder." I checked Mary Eaton and thankfully she was just knocked out. Taylor had a can of petrol which he must have planted there earlier. Mary would have been the sixth victim and gone up in flames with the lockup if Gunter hadn't been so convincing. I left the constables at the lockup until it could be securely locked, while I left in the ambulance with Mary and Taylor.

Mary recovered fairly quickly as Taylor had knocked her out with a cuff to the side of the neck. Taylor went straight into the operating theatre where the bullet was removed. I had an armed officer guard Taylor's room.

I took Mary Emery home in the officer's car and luckily her husband was in so she would be safe. After explaining to her very concerned husband I left to get a warrant to search Taylor's flat.

As it was late I would have to wait until the morning to get a warrant. I arranged to have an armed officer meet me at the station 1st thing in the morning and he could accompany me to Taylor's Flat.

I arrived home to find the lock on my front door had scratches on it. Some one had tried to pick the lock or had succeeded and may be in my house now. I walked round the outside and looked through the windows but the place was in darkness, I decided to take a chance and go in. The kitchen seemed the best entry point as it was full of things I could use for defence like saucepans and a rolling pin for example. I unlocked the door and reached in, I put the light on before grabbing a heavy frying pan.

Someone had left the drawers and cupboards open, probably looking for Constable Forward's notebook. The note book was still in my inside pocket so if that is what they were after its possible they have been waiting for me to return home. The door leading to the hall was open; I reached my hand round and put the hall light on revelling the stair cupboard open and the contents all over the hall floor. The living room was a mess to. I headed up the stairs and tried the landing light but it never came on, indicating someone had removed the bulb and was waiting in the darkness up there. As I headed for the bedroom I heard a noise behind me, I spun round as fast as I could swinging the base of the frying round in front. I just caught the sight of someone in the darkness and the frying pan struck the intruder on the side of the head sending them sprawling across the landing. I put the bedroom, bathroom and study lights on so I could get a good look at the intruder. I could make out the figure on the landing and as I walked towards the intruder my foot knocked against something on the carpet, it was the bulb for the landing light. After I replaced it I turned the light on and I felt a feeling of dread shoot through me. There lay Constable Forward with a truncheon beside her; still at least she had the headache and not me. After I handcuffed her left hand to her right ankle I telephoned the station to come and collect the unconscious constable Forward. I told them I would leave my spare front door key under my Gnome; -Albert- in the garden, and told them to inform me if she needed to go the hospital which seemed likely.

I went to Gracie Day in case she had been hurt. Gracie lived above her shop and after ringing the bell four times decided I would have to break the door in, just as I was about to bruise my shoulder a light came on and Grace opened the door after checking it was me and said, She had been fast asleep and was unaware Constable Forward had left. Gracie stood there in her emerald green dressing gown looking bleary eyed, rosy cheeked and radiant.
She was the same age as myself and for a forty five year old still very attractive.
We had been friends since school, it was only now I realised how attracted I was to her and felt a bit light headed.
She asked me in and made us both a hot chocolate drink. I asked if Constable Forward had had any visitors.

Sergeant Taylor had been round that morning to see her but that was all and no phone calls.

"Why are you looking at me like that Peter? You're giving me Butterflies."

"Sorry Grace I suddenly realise why I have never wanted a serious relationship, all this time I have felt empty as if I was waiting for someone and it was you all the time."

"I have always loved you Peter but I never thought you felt the same way; why now?"

"I was so scared Forward had killed you and the thought of not seeing you again was more than I could bear, then seeing you standing there just made me want to hold you close."

"So what's stopping you now? I have waited all these years for this moment."

I held Grace in my arms as tight as I could and felt whole and alive for the first time for years. I felt embarrassed as tears trickled down my cheeks and I suppose it was inevitable that I stayed the night.

In the morning I proposed to her and I felt ten feet tall when she said yes. I wasn't taking any chances with the food so I put it all in a big bin liner and took Grace to the supermarket and bought fresh.

She made me the best breakfast I have had since my mum's wonderful cooking.

After breakfast I headed for the station to try and get some answers from Constable Forward. I found her handcuffed to a bed in the cell. The left side of her face was red and swollen and She seemed shaken up and was trembling. I thought I would try and make out that Taylor had fingered her for the murders.

"Pull the other one sir, why would he tell you anything." She replied shakily.

"He was offered a deal if he told us every thing, all he did was pass information on to you and he was unaware that you were the killer until yesterday."

"It was the other way round, I just passed on the information to him."

"Who told you about the black Circle club? And what's so important about your diary?"

"A man phoned me and said it would lead us to the killer, it sounded a bit like Head."

"Who else is in it with you? As far I know Head, Taylor and Grainger are involved so what's the motive for killing these people."

"I don't know, Taylor was blackmailing me into passing on information because he found out I had been convicted for shoplifting when I was seventeen. He said I would be kicked out of the force and that's all I know. I was unaware about Head and Grainger's involvement in the murders or my information had anything to do with the case."

"I would imagine your record would have been overlooked as you have an excellent record. This on the other hand is another matter and you will be lucky not to get sent down."

"As far as my diary is concerned sir, I put the times dates and places I was at the time of the murders. I thought my diary was at your house and I could retrieve it before it was stolen and that was the only reason I was there, I thought you were a burglar."

"There's more in your diary than times and dates so what is so important about it."

She just sat there with a stubborn defiant look on her face and crossed her arms.

"I have it here so let's go through it again and again till we find it."

"Give me my diary, you had no right to take it, there is nothing incriminating there."

"Some one thought there was because they tried to kill you, who was it Carol, who?"

"I don't know but there was a strong smell of cigar smoke on him. It wasn't one of those three. I think he had disguised his appearance but come to think about it, his voice was the same as the one who phoned about the club. How stupid can I be I told him I had jotted his phone number in my diary and may use him again?"

"You weren't to know, where in here did you write that number? It's not on that page he phoned you, tell me and we may have our real first clue in catching him."

"Will you put in a good word for me sir? I will tell you if you do, I'm so scared."

"I will try but you're not even safe in here till we catch the killer. Hurry up or I will get you released and then you will be at his mercy and then the killer will get you out of the way."

 "It's written on the inside of the outer sleeve with other numbers, it's the bottom number, can I come with you only I feel a sitting duck in here?"

"Officer Can you handcuff yourself to Constable Forward and follow me. Keep your eyes peeled for anyone behaving suspiciously and keep you gun handy."

"I telephoned the number from my desk and to my surprise I could hear it ringing somewhere in the building but got no answer. We moved to the other end of the office and used another phone hoping to get a fix when it rang. I heard it ringing upstairs so I left it ringing and we headed up. To my disbelief it was Commander Susan Harrison's office. We headed for the Chief, Alistair Dove to update him and ask about the commander. As luck would have it he was in and to my dismay he was smoking a large expensive cigar.

"Sorry to disturb you sir. I need to get a warrant to search Sergeant Taylor's flat, I thought you could hurry things up."

"Leave Taylor to me and as for You Constable I want you in the cells for the night."

"Some one was inquiring about the Commander sir is she in today?"

"I believe she has gone to Jersey on holiday, a couple of weeks I think she said."

"Thank you Chief, I will get Constable Forward to the cells and if you would keep me updated about Sergeant Taylor please, I will keep my phone on if you need me."

The chief nodded and we left his office.

I was getting paranoid as he was smoking a large cigar and he wanted to take control of the suspects, why? Perhaps I am wrong but I felt Constable Forward, Sergeant Taylor and Gunter could be the next victims.

We made our way back to my desk and I asked the officer and Constable Forward to wait in the hall out of earshot. I phoned Miss Annie Draper, now married so now she's Mrs Annie Young and warn her that the Commander was on or on her way to the island of Jersey. Annie said that the commander had phoned her and told her to stay there as she would be arriving that evening. I told her to book out immediately and tell the reception that her and her husband had to return home urgently. I would arrange for a hire car to be waiting for them at "The Press Gang Inn" 100yds from the ferry port. I hired the car in the names of Mr Dick Ham & Miss May Sand. I told them before taking the car draw plenty of cash from a cash machine then drive to the railway station two miles away. They were to put the keys to the car in an envelope and address it to =Angle bakery= and leave it at the lost and found, I told them to buy a ticket to London with cash then get off somewhere in between and never use their bank cards on any account and just use the false names.

The armed officer that was with us was fairly new to the force and very keen so I felt he could be trusted. After getting

Gunter from the cell I drove them all to the hospital and against the doctors advice I took Sergeant Taylor. I drew £500 out of my bank which I hoped to claim back later.

I have a very good friend in charge of an army training camp on the out skirts of London and apart from being one of my old school chums we went around together in our teens. I had saved his sister from a jail sentence so I hoped he would help as he owed me that favour. Before heading for the army camp I stopped to use a public telephone. My friend Matthew, -Colonel Sanders- was surprised to hear from me and to my delight he agreed to help.

At the camp he showed us to a spare hut used by new recruits. The hut was kitted out with bunk beds and toilets but no kitchen. Colonel Sanders said he would arrange to have food sent over and informed my armed officer Jimmy Sail he would have an army uniform sent over for him and insisted he must hide his police uniform. Colonel Sanders said he would get into civvies and follow me back to the railway station to off load the hire car, which we did.

My officer constable Sail and an Army Sergeant who was about the size of a large Grizzly Bear, they called T Rex kept watch over my prisoners.

When we returned the three suspects had said nothing from the outset and barely made contact with each other.

Each one of them was handcuffed to a bunk bed next to each other but now I needed some answers.

"Taylor I will start with you, I know you are taking your orders from someone else, it will be a secret you will take to your grave if you don't tell me."

"Are you threatening me sir? You haven't got the guts."

"I was referring to the killer getting you out of the way like he did Grainger."

T Rex asked what Taylor had done. I told him he had killed two women and three men. He went berserk, grabbing Taylor by the lapels and lifting him and the end of the bed clean off the floor.

"You two get out and leave me alone with this piece of trash, just for ten minutes and I will beat the truth out of him."

"Sorry I can't let you do that Sergeant and he knows that."

As I finished speaking a hand landed on my shoulder, it was Matthew.

"My Sergeant's wife was murdered and I would not recommend you try and stop him, you and your officer wait outside."

He escorted us outside and winked at us. Officer Sail was out of his depth and looked confused.

"What's going on sir? This can't be right. I will get the sack."

"You are following orders so don't worry; I think, well I hope my friend here is just trying to help us get information out of Taylor."

"Don't worry old T Rex has never been married the Army is his wife."

All we could hear was Taylor cry out for help then silence, fearing the worst we started to go back in. Matthew grabbed my arm and shook his head. I looked at Officer Sail who looked as concerned as I was. After a few minutes the door opened and T Rex beckoned us in. Taylor was lying on the floor still handcuffed to the bed and looking white as a sheet, his whole body trembling.

Forward and Gunter looked scared and kept looking at each other.

I turned to talk to Matthew but he had gone, instead two MPs stood in the doorway.

"There's no need for that, they are hand cuffed to the bed." I remarked.

"We have come for you and your officer. You will stay in the guard house until the Sergeant has finished with them, let's go."

"Wait! Don't go, I will tell you what you want to know." Taylor cried in desperation.

T Rex picked up Taylor bodily off the floor without the slightest effort. This was no mean feat as Taylor was six foot and well built.

"You had better you piece of filth."

T Rex shouted in Taylor's face as he dropped him on the bunk.

"Would you two MPs escort the other two out while I talk to Taylor Please?"

Matthew appeared in the doorway and nodded to the MPs in agreement and sat down on a bunk to watch.

T Rex stood and glared at Taylor.

"I never took part in the murders, in fact I put two and two together and come up with Grainger and I knew he used to work with drugs, I went to the club to see if he knew or was involved in the murders. The Chiefs car was in front of the club so I turned in the drive and drove away. Later the chief called me to his office and said if I told anyone he was at the club he would make my family suffer. The next day Grainger was dead."

"You knocked out Mary Emery and pulled a gun on us at the lockup so don't give me that load of rubbish. You must think I'm stupid."

"Miss Emery was looking through the drawers when she had a call, I heard her say yes chief it's just inside the door; I looked and saw the can of petrol. The gun was hers, she drew it but I was quick and knocked her out. I tried to see what she was looking for in the drawers, which is when you surprised me. I thought you were the Chief."

"Where does Gunter fit into all this? Just seems to convenient Head getting killed."

"I took his wallet to see if I could get a lead to anyone else involved. His bank card was in the name of Colin Harrison not Colin Head. I started to work with Constable Forward as we wanted to get background information on The Chief and Colin Head."

"So why didn't you come to me and tell me all this?"

"The Chief may have found out and my family would have been in danger."

"What did you dig up about the Chief and Head?"

"You won't believe this but Head is married to the Commander. Her maiden name is Dove but you stopped me before Carol could tell me any more."

"So where does Gunter fit into all this? I need to know if he's involved."

"Better ask Carol she is the one that dug all this up about them."

Taylor was lead away and Constable Forward brought in.

"I understand you uncovered quite a bit about the chief, the Commander and Head."

"Yes Sir. Head or should I say Mr Harrison, being the Commander's husband is the brother in law of the Chief.   The Commander is the Chiefs sister. I think I know what the motive is but haven't found out anything about Gunter yet."

"Five people are dead, it escapes me what could warrant that, unless they had all found out something which seems very unlikely. Well tell me what you think is the motive."

"I think the victims all from the court were to cover up the real intended victim, Annie Draper the Stenographer. It took a lot of digging on the internet but I found a link. Annie Draper's father owns a big corporation and is terminally ill."

"You have lost me, how does that connect with the case?"

"Mr Draper's first wife bore him a daughter Susan who married Harrison, his wife sadly died in childbirth. He married again and had Annie draper, his second wife died four years ago."

"I see. If Annie is out of the way Susan Harrison cops a fortune."

"I heard through the grape vine sir that Mary Emery from Forensics was having an affair with the Chief, so that's the connection there but where Gunter comes into the plot I haven't worked out yet."

"Well if you leave with these gentlemen I will get them to bring in Gunter."

The MPs brought Gunter in and removed Constable Forward. Gunter looked scared. He kept glancing at T Rex standing by the bed with his arms crossed looking menacing.

"Well Ted Gunter, perhaps you can go over how and why you shot Colin Head and see if a hardened army man like the Sergeant, agrees with your instincts."

Gunter told his story in front of the sergeant and when he had finished T Rex asked me if he could be alone with Gunter. I agreed and everyone left and waited outside until T Rex appeared again a few minutes later.

"He is all yours now, and wants to come clean."

"Thank you Sergeant I could do with you on the force."

Gunter was looking totally demoralised and drained, maybe what T Rex had said.

"Well Mr. Gunter you're the missing link so let's get this mess cleared up."

"I was approached by Head and he told me he was promoting a new product and said he would pay me £10 for each pot I left with the milk. He only wanted important people to try the new product and gave me their address's which turned out to be the victims. I left four pots; the fifth I left in my fridge because she was away on honeymoon."

"So when did you catch on that you were involved in the murders?"

"Not until my boss Mr Curd told me the police asked who delivered to the addresses of the victims. The penny dropped so when I shot Mr Head it was to save you and vengeance for killing those people, they had always been friendly to me."

"A friendly piece of advice is stick to saving my life and leave the vengeance bit out or you will end up with a long jail sentence for murder, Have you still got the fifth pot?"

"Yes and if you hadn't gone to the dairy that day I would have eaten it myself so in fact you unknowingly saved my life too, what happens now?"

I need signed statements from all of you. I will have to contact Scotland Yard to get them involved until we return, It would be too dangerous to return until we know who our Chief of police has on his payroll, we will stay here until Scotland Yard gives us the all clear, best to be safe than sorry."

It took nearly the whole of the next day to get the statements and dossiers together. Instead of using the telephone I sent a copy of the statements and information about the motives etc, also a letter stating we would come out of hiding once I hear through the media that the guilty parties have been arrested.

One thing I will say about Scotland Yard, once one of their own has made them look corrupt they go all out to clean up the mess and to try and keep public confidence.

Four days later after the all clear the Colonel dropped us all off at the police station. We were met by a squad sent from

London. The Chief, Commander and Mary Emery received stiff sentences, Mr Gunter got six months for withholding evidence but this was squashed for saving my life. Constable Forward had her dream come true by being made up to Inspector for her outstanding work and Sergeant Taylor became our new chief of Police. I retrieved the fifth yoghurt pot and the deadly seeds which you tip into the yoghurt.

The label read '**Special promotion pack containing seeds, vitamins and herbs which will make you feel alert and full of vitality within two hours or we will award you a year's supply. Tip them in and swallow, don't chew, it will change your life**.'

Well it certainly did that, it ended it.

I was promoted to chief Inspector and I paired up with Inspector Forward on most of our cases, this led us to becoming good friends. Gracie Day and I got officially engaged.

Annie Young, 'formally Draper' left the court as a stenographer and took a part time job at her fathers company until he died, leaving her everything. She sold his company and bought herself a shop and opened a secretarial agency.

To my delight I received two tickets from Bill Potter for a play he was starring in, Gracie and I totally enjoyed it, I asked him to autograph our programmes as I new he would be famous one day.

I was right he went on to be an actor in films. We became good friends and he always sent me complimentary tickets. With Taylor in charge of our station everyone enjoyed their job.

Until I return with another Case

Be Good

Chief Inspector Peter Stewart

CHIEF INSPECTOR PETER STEWART'S

CASE 2

ACCUSED FALSELY

Chief Inspector Peter Stewart

My Second Case

Accused Falsely

A handbag finally uncovers murder, Theft and
Adultery; chaos is the result along the way, it is up
to me to unravel the mystery behind the mysterious
handbag.

ACCUSED FALSELY

I arrived at "Woodland Grange" to investigate a possible attempted murder. The Grange was a big grey rambling place forbidding and surrounded by woods, the trees swayed throwing the moonbeams across the building. The flashing lights from the police cars and the presence of the police officers warded off a lot of the eerie feeling.

I met a Constable and accompanied him to the first floor bathroom where the incident happened. As I entered the bathroom I saw a young man lying on his back on the floor and a paramedic was attending to his head wound, It would appear he had just had a shower as he was still wet and had a towel round his lower half, the man was unconscious and had a big bump on the side of his head and on the floor were the remains of a large smashed china vase.

"Mrs Cheviot; the victim's wife is in the drawing room chief Inspector with a woman officer." exclaimed the Constable.

"Thank you, I haven't met you before constable and I like to know peoples names, so if you could enlighten me I would be grateful."

"Sorry chief Inspector, I am Constable Bart White and the woman constable with the victim's wife is Constable Brenda Sky, the man is Paul Cheviot aged 28 and his wife's name is Cherry aged 30"

I followed Constable White to the drawing room, Constable Sky was comforting Mrs. Cheviot, a slim attractive woman with shoulder length blond hair, She was trembling and looking very worried. I felt like telling her to get her mascara from the same place as my fiancé Gracie as hers had run down her cheeks looking like war paint, obviously cheap old rubbish and not waterproof. A paramedic was attending to a cut on Mrs. Cheviot's hand. It serves her right that was a beautiful vase, I beckoned Constable Sky over.

"I am Chief Inspector Stewart. Have you found out the details of what happened to make her attack her husband?"

"She hasn't said anything since she called an ambulance."

"I think it's fairly obvious she did it I just need to know why."

As the Paramedic was nearly finished I waited then called him over while Constable Sky returned to Mrs. Cheviot. "Hello I am Chief Inspector Stewart; can you tell me your findings referring to the injuries inflicted on both of the occupants?" "Hello yes, I am Andy Page, the husband may have a fractured skull and most certainly has concussion, he is still unconscious so we must get him to hospital as soon as possible. Mrs. Cheviot must have sustained her injuries at the time of impact and she's lucky, just half inch to the left and it would have slashed the artery on her wrist."

"Thank you Mr. Page I had better leave you to get Mr Cheviot to hospital and many thanks, I will have a word with Mrs. Cheviot."

Mrs. Cheviot was trembling, crying and shaking her head from side to side. I noticed a decanter of brandy on the sideboard so I took her a glass.

"Hello Mrs. Cheviot I think you should drink this I just want to find out what led up to you hitting your husband over the head with the vase.

I must warn you that anything you say may be incriminating and used against you in a court of law. If you would you prefer to have a lawyer present we can continue this at the station but at present any further action would be up to your husband."

"I just lost my temper and grabbed the first thing to hand; it was the big vase in the bathroom, I was going to put dried flowers in. I never meant to hurt him, I love him very much."

"You smashed a lovely vase and tried to kill him, how much have you got him insured for Mrs. Cheviot?"

"Dam the insurance money I want him alive, he is still alive though, say he is, Please say he is I just lost my mind I was so frightened."

"Your husband has a very serious head wound and the paramedics are rushing him to hospital so how much is he insured for?"

"£37.000 but I never tried to kill him, what would be the point if I was in prison, you must believe me."

"Just tell me what happened so I can make my own mind up."

"It all started when we were shopping in Maidstone, we had had some lunch in a café and then walked round the shops; I noticed an antique shop down an ally and while we were browsing in the shop I noticed a lovely

Black Leather Handbag with a Ruby Red Velvet lining, It was priced at £89. When the shop keeper saw I was put off by the price he let me have it for £49. He must have known it was bad luck that's why he let me have it cheaper; I wish I had never bought it. The very first day I used it Paul and I started to have blazing arguments."

"What were the arguments about and where does the bag fit in?"

"We were invited to a party at Lord Quentin's place so I decided to wear my lovely Ruby Necklace; I put the necklace and purse in my new handbag and left it on the hall table while I fetched my coat, I put my coat on in front of the hall mirror then opened my new handbag to put my necklace on but it was gone"

"Are you saying your husband stole it or was someone else there?"

"My Paul was standing by the hall table when I put my bag on it containing the necklace and he was still there when I returned from the cloakroom seconds later."

"So what did your husband have to say about its disappearance?"

"He swore he never touched the bag and it was always in his sight"

"When was this today and have you found your necklace?"

"That was two weeks ago, I wore my Emerald necklace to the party and while Paul and I were dancing I had my left arm against his hip and felt something hard against my wrist, I put my hand in his jacket pocket and pulled out my Ruby necklace, He still swore he hadn't taken it."

"What has that got to do with today's attack or can't you let it drop?"

"Two days later I put £500 in the bag to pay for our long weekend break but when I got to the Travel Agents the money was gone."

"Carry on, you have my complete attention."

"I paid by cheque and when I got home Paul was counting it out on the hall table, he said he found it in his jacket pocket."

"Is your husband suffering from any illness? Do you think he is taking things from your bag for his own gain or are you putting things in his pocket just to pick on him?"

"Perhaps your henpecked Inspector but Paul certainly is not and he certainly does not need the money, anyway what would he want with my mother's old watch? It's not worth anything and he knows it so it's not for gain, perhaps he wants me committed."

"What are you talking about? So far you told me he took a Ruby necklace and £500 from your bag and before you answer wipe your face you look stupid just like a little girl who's been playing with her mum's makeup."

She glared at me and wiped her face with a wet flannel which she threw at me hitting me square in the middle of my face.

"Thanks a bunch Mrs Cheviot, carry on." I said as I threw the flannel in the sink.

"A week later I decided to get my mothers old watch mended as one of the hands had come off and the clasp on the strap had broken, I put the watch in my bag and Paul and I went out to the car, I was going to drive so I asked Paul to hold my bag while I got the car keys out of my pocket, I just can't figure out how he did it because when he handed it back seconds later, I opened my bag to get a tissue and the watch had gone, the bag was never out of my sight."

"Don't tell me you found it in your husbands pocket Mrs. Cheviot? Do you expect me to believe all this rubbish you're throwing at me?"

"It's all true Chief Inspector the watch was in his jacket pocket and how he could stand there and lie really infuriates me; he was the only one that could have taken it."

"So much so you wanted to kill him but why wait another week?"

"I was convinced he was trying to drive me insane to start with but tonight I was convinced he was trying to kill me."

"Will you get to the point and tell me why you hit him."

"I always carry my Nitro-lingual pump spray in my handbag as I suffer from angina attacks. I was having a bad attack so I went to take the spray from my bag but it was gone, I went to the bathroom to ask him where it was, this made him get out the shower in a violent rage. He said he has had enough of my paranoia; he took his jacket off the door and threw it at me. The pain in my chest was getting worse so in desperation I grabbed his jacket and found my spray in his pocket. I used the spray and as I did he glared at me, he turned back towards the shower saying he would have me committed. I was scared and panicked, all that went through my mind was he had hidden it so I would have a heart attack and die."

"I will have to have you taken into custody until your husband can verify your story; Constable Sky will escort you to the station."

"This bag has brought me nothing but trouble so if you would like it Constable Sky, please take it with my blessing."

"Would that be ok Inspector Stewart or would it be a bribe?"

"I think it will be evidence Constable Sky that's if Mrs. Cheviot is telling the truth." We left the forensics at the scene and left for the police station.

When we arrived at the station, Mrs Cheviot had a drink and then taken to a cell for the night. I checked her handbag first and left her nitro spray, tissues and address book in her bag removing her comb etc.

It was late that night when I had finished my report when Sergeant Reed informed me Mrs. Cheviot was having a heart attack, I quickly phoned for an ambulance then rushed to her cell, the first thing I did was open her bag for the spray but it had gone. Sergeant Reed remembered Miss Trend the interpreter always kept a spare Nitro-lingual spray in her desk as she suffers from angina as well and came to work without it one day.

Sergeant Reed was soon back and quickly administered it. Mrs Cheviot was in a daze and in a state of panic for about ten minutes. As she composed herself I asked her where she had hidden her spray as I personally had put it in her bag, before I could get any sense out of her the Paramedics appeared and rushed her to the hospital. Following the ambulance I kept wondering what her husband would say when he came to.

At the hospital I went to Mr. Cheviot to see if he had regained consciousness but no such luck. Feeling rather stupid I asked the sister if I could see his jacket and she agreed, what did I find? The Nitro spray. I carefully picked it up in a tissue, as I had to prove to myself that it was not the same one I had put in the bag back at the station. If it were the same one it would have the smudge of makeup on it but it hadn't.

I returned to the station and I took the Nitro spray to Mrs. Cheviot. I picked up her handbag and put my watch inside, closed it, waited two minutes then opened it to find my watch was still there.

"Perhaps I should get you checked out by a psychiatrist Mrs Cheviot because I think you had two sprays and left one in your husband's jacket before hiding the one I left in your bag."

"You're a stupid idiot inspector, why don't you believe me? Leave me alone and go and direct the traffic because you don't seem very good at crime."

"You're a sad case Mrs Cheviot and as for me being stupid, let's wait till your husband regains consciousness and see what he has to say."

"Yes let's, then you will see I am telling the truth."

I wondered why she was sticking to her wild story. She confessed to hitting him over the head with the vase so case solved. I will detain her until he regains consciousness.

It was the next morning when I got a call from the hospital to inform me Mr Cheviot had regained consciousness.

When I arrived at his bedside I could see he was looking groggy and in pain. "Hello Mr Cheviot I am Chief Inspector Peter Stewart, I would like your account of how you sustained your injuries, if you're up to it and I must tell you your wife is in custody on a suspected murder charge."

He smiled and shook his head from side to side then started to laugh.

"I know I have had a blow to the head but I must be having hearing problems, I thought you said you're holding my wife on an attempted murder charge, you can't be serious."

"Are you saying it was an accident Mr Cheviot? Only your wife hit you with the vase because she thought you were trying to drive her insane and when that hadn't worked you hid her medication hoping she would have a heart attack and die. She feared for her life so the attempted murder charge could be your wife's self defence."

"You must be joking Inspector my wife is confused and keeps mislaying things and for some reason she plants things in my jacket pocket and makes out I took them. First it was her necklace, then it was our holiday money and then her mothers clapped out old watch. Last night she stormed into the bathroom as I was getting out the shower, she accused me of taking her medication so I threw her my jacket and then as I turned to turn the shower off, I remember no more till I woke up here."

"Would you like to press charges against your wife? Or would you like me to bring her here so you can talk to her first?"

"I would be very grateful if you could, I need to try and understand what going on I find it very confusing."

He wasn't the only one, perhaps they are both a pair of fruitcakes and if I don't hurry up and solve this case I could become a donut.

After telephoning the police station to bring Mrs. Cheviot to the hospital I went to the side corridor to get a sandwich from the vending machine, as I was putting my money in a door to the right opened and a man in a tracksuit and trainers appeared in the doorway, unshaven and smelling like an old sock, I noticed he was clutching a plastic bin liner half full in one hand and a heavy torch in the other, I walked towards him as it was obvious to me he was stealing something, probably drugs.

"Hand me that bag and drop that torch you thief, I've caught you in the act."

I said as I walked up to him and with that he lifted the torch, as he did so I landed a good upper cut to his jaw sending him sprawling backwards into the room, I picked up the torch and shone it into the room revealing the man out cold on the floor, I tried the light switch but the bulb must have blown, just then a voice said.

"I have the new bulb here, who are you and what are you doing in the medicine room?" I turned and saw a sister holding a light bulb in her hand.

"I have just caught a thief trying to steal some drugs, I am chief Inspector Stewart and I will phone the yard and get him taken into custody."

I shone the torch on the man on the floor to revile the thief to the sister.

"You stupid blundering fool, you have just knocked out Anthony Steel the head surgeon."

"What are you talking about? That scruffy smelly thing can't be a surgeon."

"He has been on a charity run for two days but we had to call him in for an emergency operation this afternoon. He was getting the necessary drugs for the operation."

That put me right off my sandwich and after putting the light bulb in I helped the sister to get the surgeon into a wheelchair and take him to casualty.

"This idiot just knocked Mr. Steel out and he has an emergency operation later."

The sister shouted at the staff as we reached casualty, if looks could kill I would be dead, the doctors and nurses just glared at me so I apologised again and went to Mr. Cheviot's room and decided to wait for his wife to arrive.

Mr. Cheviot had fallen asleep so I sat in a chair to wait; I kept hoping the surgeon would be ok to carry out the operation. I was surprised to see Inspector Forward with Mrs. Cheviot enter the room instead of Constable Sky. Mrs. Cheviot walked over to her husband's bedside and woke him up; she hugged him and burst into tears. Inspector Forward Smiled at me.

"Hello Peter, hope you don't mind me bringing Mrs. Cheviot only I wanted to see the mysterious handbag, sounds very weird and spooky."

"Of course I don't mind you coming along always lovely to see you Carol, the handbag was with Mrs. Cheviot back at the station."

"She never had it with her when I collected her, are you sure?"

"Excuse me Mrs. Cheviot; I left the handbag in question with you back at the station, where did you put it?"

"I took my things out and gave it to Constable Sky as she really liked it." Inspector Forward was annoyed; she kicked me in my shin then left the room.

"I take it by the way you two are slobbering over each other my services are no longer required, oh! By the way Mr. Cheviot can you buy your wife some decent mascara, last time I was frightened that bad was when I saw my perspective mother in-law in her bloomers vest and curlers."

"Thank you for all your help Inspector." He said and as I was leaving the room I heard him say.

"What's he on about Cherry? You don't use curlers and you haven't got mascara on."

"Shut up Paul and move over I'm coming in bed with you."

If I had a do not disturb sign I would have hung it on the door, not that that would have made a difference as the sister was striding up the corridor towards his room.

As I was passing the reception I noticed Anthony Steel the surgeon I had mistaken for a thief coming toward me still in his tracksuit, a nurse with a big metal bedpan accompanied him. To cheer him up I said.

"You can't go to the theatre dressed like the mother-in-law on a bad day."

He went red in the face took a wide swing at me, he lost his balance and on the way down hit his head on the metal bed pan knocking himself out.

The nurse glared at me and raising the bed pan above her head started to rush towards me. A man I would have stood my ground but a female mental case with a bed pan, no way, I was out of the main doors and back to my car within seconds, I looked back to the hospital entrance and saw the nurse waving the bedpan at me and shouting obscenities. I decided to go home and have an early night and slept like a log

Next morning when I arrived at the station I asked Sergeant Sid Kemp on the desk to see if Constable Sky was in the building so I could wrap up the case.

"She sure is and I don't think she will be leaving for a while"

"Why, is she swamped with paperwork? Come on Sid don't keep me in suspense, where is she?"

"She's in the cells for grievous bodily harm; she is quite a woman chief."

Sid Kemp the Sergeant was always trying to pull my leg and I thought this was one of those times so to even things up I said.

"Ok and by the way were you hurt? Only I couldn't help but notice your passenger's wing on your car is smashed in."

He went red in the face and rushed off to the car park. Feeling good I had got my own back on him I went to the office and sat at my desk to write up the report on the Cheviots.

Sally Trent the typist came over to my desk looking concerned.

"Chief Inspector Stewart could you go and see Brenda Sky as she has been asking for you, she is very upset."

"Of course I will I was going to get her report on the Cheviot case."

"I've just finished typing it up, I'll leave it on your desk, She's in cell 3."

"What's she doing there? You mean Sergeant Kemp was telling the truth about her being charged with grievous bodily harm but what happened?"

She shrugged her shoulders and walked off back to her desk.

I had to go to the main desk for access to the cells and I apologised to Sid about pretending his car had been damaged, he smiled and said.

"You had me fooled, very convincing and I had that coming, let's go and see Brenda she is in a bit of a state and has been asking for you."

Sergeant Kemp unlocked the cell door and I slowly pushed it open to reveal Constable

Brenda Sky curled up asleep on the bunk
bed.

"Brenda; its chief Inspector Stewart, are you
awake? I'm here to help."

She lifted her head and sat up slowly
looking totally demoralised and said.

"I never meant to hurt him, just try and
arrest him for stealing my money."

"Just tell me what happened from the
beginning, I thought you were off duty last
night and you were going to a big party."

"I had a blind date with a bloke and
everything was going fine until half way
through the evening when we went to the
bar, he said he would pay but I couldn't
believe my eyes when he pulled my money
clip out of his jacket pocket."

"What made you think it was your money
clip? Surly you were mistaken."

"My name was engraved on it, it was a
present from my sister plus it was missing
out of my hand bag. He pretended he was
shocked that he had it in his pocket, in the
heat of the moment I grabbed my money
clip containing my fifty pounds and slapped
his face."

"I would hardly call that grievous bodily
harm Brenda, what a pathetic wimp he is."

"When I slapped his face he lost his balance and hit his head on the side of the bar and as he hit the ground he rolled into the legs of some people who fell on him."

"Sounds painful, was he badly injured or just angry at having his pride shattered?"

"He was unconscious when they took him to hospital and no one has let me know how he is, I need to apologise to him."

"I will phone the hospital and find out what the score is then let you know, was that the handbag Mrs. Cheviot gave you yesterday?"

"Yes; Why? I suppose she wants it back now, well I haven't got it someone stole it in the scuffle, so it was a good job my money was in my hand and not in my handbag."

"If it was still in your bag none of that would have happened, would it? And no she does not want the bag back in fact she was glad to see the back of it; I think it's fairly safe to say your date was innocent."

"My date was Trevor Hand and there is no way he will believe that the bag put it in his pocket, he will think I put my money and clip in his jacket."

"Sergeant Kemp I am going to take Brenda to the hospital in my custody and I am disgusted that she was locked up in the first place."

"Don't blame me it was Jack Taylor the chief, he thought it would look like favouritism if he had treated her differently, he said she was only going to be here for a couple of hours just for show."

"Sorry Sid I should have known you would have handled it differently, still I suppose the chief was right, well Brenda are you coming?"

She smiled and headed out of the cell door followed by Sid and myself.

"Give us fifteen minutes before you tell the chief Sid just in case he disagrees and wants her returned."

"Sergeant Kemp nodded, patted Brenda on the shoulder and we left for the hospital wondering what her date would do about the incident.

A sister was just leaving Mr Hand's room when we arrived.

"Hello! Sister I am Chief Inspector Stewart; how is Mr. Hand nothing serious I hope? "

"Apart from a headache he has bruised ribs and backache, he is awake you can go in."

The Sister smiled and walked off.

I opened the door to reveal Mr. Hand sitting up in bed, when he saw Brenda his face lit up and he put his arms out to her for a hug. "I suppose the blow to your head has affected your mind Mr. Hand, I would have decked her."

Mr. Hand thought that was funny until he started to laugh and hurt his ribs.

Brenda and Mr. Hand hugged and kissed and then Brenda pulled up a chair and sat down at his bedside holding his hand.

I explained about the bag and how things mysteriously disappear from the bag and then end up in the man's pocket that the woman is with.

Brenda apologised for accusing him and for causing his injuries, she told him he could move in with her until he was well just to make up for the incident and as a way of an apology.

"I am going to leave before you two start slobbering over each other and if I were you Mr. Hand I would get checked out as soon as possible and take Brenda up on her offer, then you can have a bit more privacy, as for the charges against you Constable Sky they never existed, Good luck you two and I'm off back to the yard."

"Thank you Chief Inspector I will take Brenda up on her offer and will be the perfect gentlemen so don't worry she will be completely safe."

"Don't be stupid Mr. Hand, withdraw that statement about being a perfect gentleman or she is likely to withdraw her offer."

He looked shocked and Brenda went red in the face, big smiles appeared on their faces as they nodded at me in agreement.

As I was leaving the hospital I noticed a man struggling to get out of his car so I went over to him and helped him out, as he stood up I noticed a big bump on his forehead and bad bruising round his eyes, he wore an expensive suit and drove a big Jaguar, I reached into the car and got his briefcase but as I handed it to him I realised it was the surgeon I had mistaken for a thief, I turned to go before he recognised me but as I did so he grabbed me by the shoulder.

"Wait! Would you mind helping me into the hospital please I would be grateful, I feel a bit light headed."

He had his head tilted downwards so he had not recognised me, without speaking I took his briefcase and helped him through the main doors.

I took him over to reception and put his briefcase on the desk. He looked up saw it was me and grabbing his briefcase swung it at me in a circular motion, missing me it did full circle knocking the receptionist flying. The Surgeon lost his balance fell on his back and was out cold again.

Two nurses who had witnessed the incident came rushing to his side and the receptionists aid followed by a security man.

"I saw the whole thing on my monitor, you're Chief Inspector Stewart, glad to meet you and all I can say is he must have had a brain storm, I can't think why he attacked you like that."

"I will let you explain what happened as you saw it all, fancy attacking me after I helped him out of his car and into the hospital, still I meet a lot of weirdo's in my job."

I quickly left and headed back to the station and on the way I noticed a man grab a young woman outside a jewellery store, I pulled over but before I got to them the man handed the bag back and the woman ran off. I followed the man into the shop and asked him what had just occurred.

"The woman was a known shop lifter and I spotted her putting a pocket watch in her handbag but when I looked in the handbag there was just a small purse, keys, a lighter and a packet of cigarettes, there was no way she could have removed the watch from the bag and she looked as shocked as I was to see the watch had disappeared, do you think it was some sort of magic trick, like slight of hand?"

"You could be right, I recognised the woman she is Heather Main and I will go round to her address and have a word, we have apprehended her before and if I recover the watch I will get it returned to you."

"Thank you Inspector it was worth £4075 as it was a solid gold antique."

"Can you describe the handbag as I was to far away to get a good look?"

"Yes it was a good quality black leather bag with a dark red velvet lining."

It was easier to agree with him than try and explain what had really transpired.

I made my way to Heather Main's address at 19 Weldon Flats, the lights in the flat were on when I arrived but I got no answer but when I looked through the kitchen window I spotted Heather lying on the floor apparently unconscious.

The small window of the kitchen was open so I leaned through and opened the side window and climbed through, Heather had a black eye and was partly conscious muttering.

"He has taken it and left me, please help." I managed to get her up and sat her on a chair at the kitchen table.

"What Happened? Heather it's me Chief Inspector Stewart, remember I brought you home the last time you were arrested and let you off with a caution and that was a waste of time as you've have been at it again."

"You can't arrest me because I never left that jewellers with anything ask at the shop if you don't believe me, you've been made a chief wow and who did you bribe to get promoted"

"Very funny, anyway Mr. Drake who owns the jewellers defiantly saw you put the watch in your bag so where is it? Be honest with me and I will try to help you."

"I can't explain it but when I got back here my boyfriend John asked what was wrong, he said I looked out of breath and very worried, I told him what had happened and he produced the watch from his jacket saying he suddenly felt a weight in his pocket about ten minuets before I arrived home, it was the same watch, I told him everything then he hit me left with the watch and the handbag."

"Where is he now? I need to take the handbag back to the station."

"I don't know where he's gone, John believes in the supranational and thinks the handbag has powers."

"His second name wouldn't be Saunders by any chance?"

"Yes how did you know? He said he has just moved here from Wales."

"He's just got out from a six year jail sentence and the reason I knew who he was is because he drove the prison mad with his ranting of witchcraft and the paranormal, in fact he thinks he's a warlock."

"What was he in jail for? Only he was nice when I first met him but he started to frighten me with his violent temper, it's not the first time he has hit me and I'm scared to finish with him in case he kills me."

"Burglary to start with and then mugging, he wasn't happy just robbing people he had to beat them up, the last victim nearly died."

"I can't stay here in case he comes back; could you give me a lift to my friends place please because he doesn't know she lives?"
"Be glad to at least I will know where you are, do you know where he's staying or know of any friends he has?"
"He stays here most of the time but sometimes at Sandy's place who's his best mate he has known from school."
"Sandy Sloan! She used to be his ex girlfriend before he went inside, she's another nasty piece of work and they are both on parole. Get your things together before he returns."
"What a louse he told me his mate Sandy was a man, I'll get my things."
While Heather was packing her case I phoned the station for two officers to watch her flat in case he returned, Heather had not given him a key so he would have to break in then Saunders could be arrested and sent back to jail. Good job she hadn't told me where her friend lived before I agreed to give her a lift, I would have told her to catch a bus as her friend lived fifteen miles the other side of Maidstone.
After dropping Heather off I returned to the station, to find out the address of Sandy

Sloan and get the bag back to stop this trail of chaos.

Inspector Forward was in the office and she agreed to find the address for Sandy Sloan while I grabbed a sandwich and coffee. I had just finished my snack when Inspector Forward put a crime report in front of me. A woman in her mid thirties with short sandy coloured hair and roughly six feet tall had been apprehended for suspected shoplifting, the security guard had let her go owing to the fact that nothing was found on her person.

"Carol! That has got to be Sandy Sloan they certainly never wasted any time putting the bag to use."

"I recognised her description straight away chief and here is her address."

"That's very apt, 11 Sandstone Terrace, Sandy Lane, Perhaps it would be a good idea if we took Bulldozer and Mammoth with us to handle Taylor."

"Sergeant Green and Constable Arnold would be the best choice I agree, one look at them and I would imagine Saunders would give up without a fight, if he had any sense."

"That's what I thought, even my ex drunken mother in law would think twice but there again I have never seen her back down from a fight especially wearing her hobnailed boots."

"You've never liked your mother in law, I remember the time you took her car keys out of her handbag, left her car further up the road on double yellow lines before putting them back. In a way you were responsible for the traffic wardens broken jaw."

"So I was stupid and I hope she never finds out it was me, my EX! Mother-in-law."

"What about the time you pinned a plastic cup on the back of her coat with a sign; <u>I AM STUPID PLEASE GIVE GENOURESLY.</u>
She really laid into those three young men for laughing at her."

"You're a really good friend Carol for not telling, anyway I have changed now."

"I hope so; your life wouldn't be worth living if she found out."

"Point taken and I will cancel the ton of manure I arranged to have dumped in her front garden, that's if I am not too late."

"Take that stupid grin off your face chief While I round up the boys."

It was lucky I sent cash to the manure company and a false name because I was too late, still if she does grow beautiful roses I wouldn't mind taking some off her hands for Gracie. Carol soon returned with the lads and we set off for 11 Sandstone Terrace.

We parked a little way up the lane where we got a good view of Sandy's front door but after ten minutes I had to ask Sergeant Green, alias 'Bulldozer' to open his window as his aftershave was making us feel nauseous. As he opened his window a car pulled up on the drive of number eleven, Sandy Sloan and John Saunders emerged from the car and in Saunders hand was a carrier bag which I assume held the spoils. Inspector Forward parked behind Sloan's car to block any escape. The lads kicked the front door open and rushed in followed by ourselves, as Carol and I entered the kitchen we were greeted by the sight of Saunders out cold on the floor and with Bulldozer towering over him, Sandy Sloan's head was in the washing up bowl and being held down by Constable Arnold alias Mammoth, she was kicking her legs about desperately trying to escape.
"I think you can let her up now Constable" Inspector Forward went to take over but when Constable Arnold released his grip Sandy Sloan turned her head covered in

soap suds and grabbed a knife, she tried to stab Carol but Constable Arnold quickly decked her. After hand cuffing them we looked in the carrier bag to find it contained items of jewellery. We searched the house and car for the handbag without any luck. As Bulldozer picked Saunders up off the floor I searched Saunders jacket pockets just in case he had more spoils he was not going to declare to Sloan. I was right because there in his right pocket was an Emerald studded broach. The only reason they would have come back without the bag would be if someone at the last shop they had stolen from snatched the bag from her. That person would have thought the broach was still in the bag. It is still out there and that spells trouble for someone.

I left Sergeant Green and Inspector Forward to take Sloan and Saunders into custody while Constable Arnold stayed behind at the property for the carpenter to arrive and secure the front door.

Back at the station I went straight to my desk and checked the tags on the jewellery, they clearly came from different shops but the main one to find would be the one the broach was taken from and hopefully find the mysterious handbag.

The tag on the broach had the initials C.P. and number 17438.

The only jewellers in the phone book with those initials were Cyril Price, so I set off with the bag of spoils.

Mr Price was over the moon to get the brooch back, when he snatched the handbag from Sloan and found nothing inside he threw it at their car as it sped away up the road. A member of the public must have picked up the bag and it had disappeared and eluded me once again, Mr Price helped me identify where the other jewellery came from so I took his statement as I did with the other jewellers.

It took me two hours to write up the report and by this time I was tired and drained by the day's events and was nearly dead on my feet. I decided to go home for a bite to eat and forty winks.

I never like lying in bed in the day it gives me a morbid feeling so after a bite to eat and a coffee I decided to lie on the settee. It felt like heaven as my head sunk into the soft cushion and my body started to feel as light as a passing cloud. Now totally detached from my body all I had left was my mind.

I started daydreaming about being rich enough to buy a nature reserve, as I drove through the gates of the reserve instead of a Rolls Royce I was in my old Sierra and a feeling of great contentment washed over me like a cool breeze on a hot summer's day, but when I opened the glove compartment to get my binoculars I was greeted by a cobra, exiting the car at great speed I turned and was face to face with a snorting Rhino, its great big pointed horn pressing against my nose.

I woke up with a start and my headache, aches and pains flooded back like an angry sea. As I was swallowing some strong painkillers I decided to go and pick up Mrs. Cheviot, I wanted her to show me where she had purchased the handbag and try to find its origin.

She was far from happy when I turned up on her doorstep and given a choice of returning to the station for further questioning or a quick trip to the shop she picked the shop. Walking down the archway to the shop seemed a bit eerie as the only lights were from the shop windows and being 5.15pm some had already closed and turned their lights off which made the archway dark and forbidding.

The antique shop was still open so in we went. The owner was a short stocky man with thick ginger hair and he wore what looked like a brown velvet smoking jacket with thick brown corduroy trousers and brown Swede shoes, making him look like an antique himself. I introduced myself and asked if he remembered selling the lady the handbag which he did but the main thing I wanted to know was the history behind it. All he new was a Lady Winter had brought it in with other items and luckily he had taken her address.

As Mrs. Cheviot had to get home to make her husband his dinner before he arrived home at seven PM, I dropped her home before heading off to Lady Winter's home for some enlightenment.

I admit I expected a big manor house but instead a quaint little cottage greeted me, which I would have fancied living in myself. Lady Winter was I imagine around her late sixties and well preserved, also well spoken with short golden hair, probably a colour rinse, she sported a pale green costume consisting of a jacket, knee length skirt and a string of peach pearls draped over her white silk blouse and wearing white shoes, anyway that is enough about her its time for me to get some answers.

"Sorry to bother you Lady Winter I am Chief Inspector Peter Stewart and if I may come in I would like to ask you some questions, it's about the handbag you sold recently."

"Please come in and join me in a cup of Earl Grey."

"No thanks I think that is an acquired taste but a strong black coffee would be nice."

"I don't like it either so I will join you in a black coffee; I cannot stand Earl Grey I keep it for guests."

"I guess you offer it to your guests for snob value, how sad is that?"

"No need to be impertinent **Chief Inspector!** But I guess you are right."

She wasn't a bad sort in fact she was very down to earth or so she seemed.

"Did the handbag belong to you Lady Winter as strange things have happened to people who have come into contact with it?"

"I'm not sure what you mean by strange things but it belonged to my daughter, it bought her nothing but bad luck and in fact it seemed to be responsible for her marriage break up."

"Could I have a word with your daughter, as she could clear up this mystery?"

"Angie is in prison for grievous bodily harm because something happened concerning the handbag, she said it was possessed and was responsible."

"I take it that it was her husband she inflicted the bodily harm to, I would like to talk to him as well, mainly to help him understand what transpired."

"You can try but he is still suffering from a head injury and he has not been able to tell his side of the incident, Barry was punched in the face by my daughter Angie when they were having an argument at the top of their stairs, Barry my son in law lost his balance and fell down the stairs hitting his head on a brass umbrella stand in the lobby at the bottom, Angie phoned the ambulance who intern phoned the police, the umbrella stand was lying beside him with his blood on it."

"So the police jumped to the wrong conclusion and said she had hit him over the head with it, then they dismissed her version that he fell down the stairs."

"That's right Chief Inspector, My son in-law Barry Peck has a back injury which her lawyer said backed up her story and could only have been caused by him falling down the stairs, which was ignored."

"If you write the name of the prison your daughter is being detained in and the hospital your son in-law is in I will pay them a visit, if you can remember who was in charge of the case that would be a great help?"

"I think his name was Inspector Saunders but I can't be sure; I phoned the hospital to inquire how Barry was but they said he had not been admitted there; I did hear one of the ambulance drivers mention Dark Chimneys."

I took the address of the prison and thanked her for her help. I phoned the station to find out Dark Chimneys address.

I found Dark Chimneys which was a big old grey sandstone place and looked more like a fifties mental institute, it was situated out in the sticks and looked a bit neglected with ivy covering most of the building and to gain entry I had to pull a rusty bell chain in the front porch and a loud clang rang out, I expected Boris Karloff to answer the door but instead a small thin woman with grey hair and wearing a sisters' uniform stood in the doorway.

"Hello I am Chief Inspector Peter Stewart and I need to see Barry Peck."

With out a word she beckoned me to follow her after slamming the big old oak door shut and sliding three large bolts across.

"The front door looks very secure and even the mother in-law would be hard pressed to get through there but then again she's capable of anything."

I looked at her and smiled. The old sister looked at me without a single expression on her face; she turned and carried on down the corridor. A shrivelled up old misery guts and what a dump. The ceilings were high, in-fact about nine feet tall and covered in cobwebs and the spiders must have sitting tenant's rights by now, dim bulbs hung down from the ceilings spaced about twenty feet apart making our shadows dance about like grey ghosts stalking us. When we reached Mr. Pecks room I was amazed at the door it was a strong thick oak door with a sliding peephole, the sister took out some deadlock keys from her pocket and unlocked the door.

"Why was the door locked sister surly he's not dangerous?"

She just beckoned me into the dimly lit room then locked the door behind her.

She stood in silence waiting for me to interview Mr. Peck, feeling very uneasy about the whole episode I walked over to his bedside.

"Mr. Peck, are you awake? I am a police officer and would like to ask you how you sustained these injuries?"

He opened his eyes and struggled to sit up; I assisted him then waited for his response.

"Before I interview you tell me why do they keep your door locked only the dumb dwarf standing in the shadows won't say?"

"The doctor told me this place is haunted and a ghost wanders the corridors at night, I told him he was talking stupid, that was until one night my door opened and a figure dressed in white and without a face appeared, it seemed to groan as if in pain then disappeared back out the door."

"Even without your head injuries this place is enough to twist your mind."

"I never imagined it and I shouted out then Sally in the next room rushed in and screamed it had also been in her room."

I turned to the sister and asked what was going on but got no answer.

"Are you dumb sister or just trying to add to the atmosphere of this dump?"

I remarked to the old woman who looked like some demented gargoyle.

"I've never heard her speak but getting back to the incident with my wife, She accused me of stealing from her and claimed she found her passport in my jacket pocket when she was sending it to the cleaners, She thought I had taken it from her handbag and hidden it in my jacket so she would miss her flight."

"Did she miss her flight?"

"Yes that's why she punched me, don't ask me how it got in my jacket unless she put it there, I really haven't got a clue what's going on."

"Your wife is being detained in prison, mainly because the police attending the scene jumped to the conclusion your wife struck you with the brass umbrella stand at the bottom of the stairs."

"Last thing I remember was we were arguing at the top of the stairs when she punched me in the face, I lost my balance and fell down the stairs; All I remember was tumbling down the stairs until I struck my head on something when I rolled into the lobby."

"How is your back now and do you think you are fit to leave this dump?"

"She won't let me leave; I can't even make a phone call."

Turning to the old lady I asked to leave and in response she stood up and unlocked the door and as she did so I took the keys from her and held her down in a chair.

"Get your cloths on Mr Peck and let's get you out of this nut house."

A loud scream bellowed from the old woman's toothless mouth bringing my hand swiftly over her shrivelled lips. Mr. Peck quickly got dressed then helped me gag the old lady by stuffing one of his socks in her mouth and tied her to the chair.

"Let's go to the next room and get this Sally out as well." I remarked but To our dismay the next room was empty, we tried all the other rooms and found Mr. Peck was the only patient in the whole place. We finally arrived at the kitchen door which was half open, a light was on and a person snoring could be heard. We carefully made our way back to the front door and made a quick exit.

As we drove away a large man and a young woman rushed out of the front door and gave chase. Mr Peck said as the two figures started shrink into the distance.

"That's Sally! She must be in on it with them, why was I put here in the first place? This is an old asylum not a hospital."

"I was told you sustained bad back injuries but I haven't seen any signs of you being in pain with your back, how did you heal so quickly?"

"My back is fine, in fact I came to as we were driving away from my home but as I came to the man who was just giving chase gave me an injection, all I remember was waking up in that room and they kept giving me injections."

"How do you feel about me dropping you off at your mother in-laws?"

"I would like that and I can't thank you enough, I don't know your name."

"I am Chief inspector Peter Stewart, I need to see your wife and find out how you ended up imprisoned in that dump, mark me there are two officers on the force that will be paying a visit to that place and they I am positive will get some answers."

We arrived at Lady Winters home and explained what had happened to Mr. Peck, her eyes filled with tears and after giving him a hug she disappeared into the kitchen to make him a decent meal as she described it.

"I am off home now and if anyone phones or calls your son in-law is not here and as far as you know he is still in hospital, I will pay a visit to your wife Mr. Peck and let you know the outcome."

Before driving off I phoned the station and left a message for Sergeant Green and Constable Arnold to make a visit to Dark Chimneys and arrest everyone on site for kidnapping but detain them in separate cells until I have interviewed them.

Feeling tired, irritable and nursing a thick headache from the days events I pulled over to an off licence grocery store for some painkillers. To my dismay a boy about 14yrs old was on his way out with a four pack of Lager, blocking the door I called for the shopkeeper.

"Why did you steal the Lager young man do you want a criminal record?"

The shopkeeper came striding towards me red in the face and angry.

"Why don't you mind your own business? How dare you call him a thief?"

I took my badge out and held it up for him to see.

"You sold spirits to an underage and you will have the book thrown at you."

"Simon's father pays for them in advance and sends Simon round to collect them, I am sorry I never meant to break the law."

"So your name is Simon, why didn't your father come and collect them?"

"I can answer that Chief Inspector, his father picks on Simon and beats him if he doesn't come and get them for him."

"The most pressing thing at the moment is painkillers so if you can sell me the strongest you have I may be able to think straight."

The shopkeeper handed me a packet and a small bottle of lemonade, I insisted on paying for them and took down the name of the shopkeeper, 'Charlie Strong' and the boy's 'Simon Tell'.

"I will take Simon home and have a word with his father but as for you Mr Strong, if you ever so much as let an under age any where near spirits and that includes cigarettes, I will make sure you go down for it, do you understand me?"

He went red in the face and nodded then I took the boy home.

Mr Tell answered the door and started shouting at the boy; I introduced myself and told him he would have to fetch his drink himself.

He grabbed the boy by the hair, I grabbed Mr. Tells wrist and put him in an arm lock then handcuffed his hands behind him.

"Is your mother in Simon? I can't leave you here on your own?"

"My mum left us last month but my auntie lives in the flat below."

"Let's get you to your Auntie's, your dad is spending the night in the cells, we need to sort out a safer living arrangement for you. After I dropped, Simon off at his Auntie's and after a struggle I managed to get Mr. Tell Locked up.

I went home to a nice hot cocoa, watched a film and fell asleep.

The next morning at the station, I told Inspector Forward she was in charge of Mr Tell's case as I was to busy tracking down the handbag. After telling Sergeant Green and Constable Arnold about my rescuing Barry Peck from the so-called hospital I sent them out there while I set off to visit Mrs. Peck in prison.

The prison Warden sent a female officer with Mrs. Peck to the interview room. Mrs Peck looked pale, very worried and sat looking at the floor and started to cry.

"Mrs. Peck my name is Chief Inspector Peter Stewart and I have seen your husband. He verifies your story and he is not pressing charges, go with the officer and collect your things then I will take you home."

She lifted her head, her sad eyes red and watery; she gave a half hearted smile and followed the warden to fetch her things

As we drove I explained that I had taken her husband to her mother in secret. Mrs. Tell was shocked to find out her husband had been kidnapped and insisted she had called the normal emergency number and had never heard of Dark Chimneys. She was either lying or there was an underlying sinister plot afoot and I was determined to find out and squash it. The reunion of Mr. and Mrs Tell at Lady Winters was very emotional, making me believe her story.

"When you two have finished slobbering over each other I need some answers, if you Lady Winter could round up some of your tasty coffee I would be very grateful."

"That's the least I can do after all you have done Chief Inspector."

"Mrs. Peck, where did you obtain the handbag your husband supposedly took your passport from? But before you answer you owe your husband an apology and not just for the blow you inflicted on him but also for you're accusations."

"I do regret every thing that I have done and I sincerely regret hitting you Barry. Chief Inspector why are you so sure Barry hadn't taken it and do you know who did put my passport in his pocket?"

"That's what you can probably tell me by informing me where you obtained the handbag."

"The property we live in is more than five centuries old and called High Firs; it housed the same family for generations and it must have belonged to one of them, it was in an old trunk in the attic."

"The handbag has caused a string of incidents, the female partner puts something valuable in it which disappears and materialises in the male's jacket. Crooks got hold of it and realising its potential used it for shoplifting jewellery."

"How weird, sorry I doubted you Barry it's all been like a bad dream."

"Can you remember the officer in charge? Your mother has given me a name; I just need to confirm it with you as it's very important."

"I am sure it was an Inspector Saunders, yes it was, as I remember it was the same surname as our post woman. He wasn't like you he was rather loud and abrupt and determined to get me locked up. He's a nasty piece of work and people like him shouldn't be in the police force."

"May I use your telephone Lady Winter I need to clear something up?"

Lady Winter nodded and I phoned my friend at the local hospital.

Mr. Harry Cooper was in charge of emergency calls and Mr Cooper claimed an ambulance was dispatched but then it was recalled by someone from the police station who stated it was a false alarm.

"Until I can get to the bottom of this Lady Winter I suggest you keep your daughter and son in-law upstairs out of sight, if any one asks about them deny all knowledge and call me straight away."

They all agreed and I set off for the station hoping to find some answers.

The first person I would be talking to would be Inspector Saunders.

Sergeant Kemp on the main desk informed me that Inspector Saunders had arrived for work but he had bumped into Sergeant Green and Constable Arnold on their way to

Dark Chimneys; he went upstairs to his desk and said he was reporting sick and left. I headed for the Chiefs office to tell him of my suspicions. Taylor I could trust as before Jack's promotion to Chief he was Sergeant Jack Taylor and proved he was trustworthy. Without hesitation he issued a warrant for Inspector Saunders arrest in case he decided to leave the country. He said he would inform me when Saunders was in custody and in the meantime the bag had turned up at a gambling casino so off I set again.

The Lucky Roulette club was a respectable club as far as casinos go; the owner Sam Cash; (that is what I thought) but that is his real name and he ran a clean joint. Two of his men held a woman accused of stealing another player's chips. She was seen putting the pile of roulette chips in her bag and refused to have her bag searched. Mr Cash called the police and the mention of a handbag assigned me to the case, I hoped it was the right bag. She was given a choice either be arrested or hand the chips back, she handed me the bag which I passed to Mr Cash.
I knew he would find nothing as it was the possessed bag I was after.

The chips had disappeared from her handbag along with her purse.

"I am sorry Inspector I defiantly saw her put the stack of chips in her handbag and the bag hasn't been out of my site, I really don't understand?"

"What have you got to say for yourself? You can start with your name."

"Why do you want my name? The only thing missing is my purse."

I pointed to odd CCTV cameras dotted about the walls indicating that she had been recorded on tape and would prove she had taken the chips.

"I take it they are recording Mr. Cash? So perhaps we could look at the footage and see where she put the chips but first where is your husband? Find him and we find the missing contents from the handbag."

"Joe is over there on the fruit machines, he's the one with the blue shirt on and grey jacket on the back of his chair."

We escorted the woman over to the man she had pointed out. I asked him to show us the contents of his jacket pockets.

"She hasn't been anywhere near him inspector your wasting your time." Exclaimed Mr. Cash.

Picking her husbands jacket off the back of his chair I handed it to him to show us the contents.

The look on their faces made me wish I had brought a camera with me.

"Can you explain how your wife's purse and those roulette chips ended up in your pocket; Mr.?"

"Joe Simons, what on earth is going on? And who are you?"

"I am Chief Inspector Stewart and this is the owner, Mr. Cash."

"What's all this about Susan? What have you done now?"

I handed the roulette chips to Mr. Cash and asked if Mr. & Mrs Simons were not welcome at the club and he nodded. After taking their address I gave them a warning that I would keep an eye on them and showed them off the premises, after confiscating the handbag as stolen property.

"Why did you let them go and how did you know the bag was stolen?"

After explaining about the handbag Mr. Cash stood there in disbelief.

Feeling great that I finally had the handbag in custody I headed back to the station in anticipation of raping up this case.

After locking it in the drawer of my desk I asked Constable Brenda Sky to look up any history on High Firs and gave her the address. I headed for the Chief's office hoping he had managed to apprehend Inspector Saunders. His office was empty so I went to Sergeant Kemp on the front desk.

"Hello Sid have you seen the chief about or Green and Arnold?"

"The Chief has gone to the airport. Green and Arnold are on their way back from that nut house with three people they arrested."

To save time I thought I would carry on and update my report on the case. The handbag may have been a headache but may have been a blessing in disguise, if I was right it has uncovered a corrupt member of the force.

I had all but finished the report when Brenda Sky came over to my desk and put a sheet of A4 paper on my desk.

"I think that's what you were looking for sir."

"Thank you, amazing how you women find these things out so quickly."

'Tall Firs' were built and occupied by a family called Harcourt; they finally sold and moved away recently after a fatality at the property.

Something was telling me I had to find out more about the fatality, I had an overwhelming feeling that it was somehow tied in with the handbag.

Sergeant Green's loud voice broke the silence followed by Constable Arnold's bulk filling the office doorway.

"We have them sir, the big bloke is a bit worse for wear, he attacked Sergeant Green and that was a bit stupid wasn't it sir?"

"Perhaps Sergeant Green should have told him his nickname was Bulldozer it could have saved him some grief."

We made our way to the cells and Constable Arnold asked.

"Would you like to interview the old lady first sir?"

"Waste of time, she is dumb as far as I know."

"Your wrong there sir, the language that came out of her mouth would embarrass your ex mother in-law, perhaps not if you know what I mean."

After being informed that co-operation would mean a lighter sentence all three opened up and dropped Inspector Saunders well and truly in it.

As I came back up from the cells the Chief was at the main desk with Saunders in handcuffs.

"Well done chief, book him for kidnapping to start with."

After he was booked and taken to the cells I filled the Chief in on what had transpired so far in this case, he was really angry that Saunders was going to hold Barry Peck for Ransom.

I remembered two previous kidnap cases that were still outstanding and they were still unsolved even though ransoms were paid. I decided to re-interview the three in the cells. It was a safe bet that Saunders was behind them and he was the Inspector in charge of those two cases but never solved them.

The Chief came with me and offered the old woman who was seventy-two a likely suspended sentence for her co-operation. She sang like a bird.

As it was now midday, the Chief took me to the canteen for lunch and discussed the next move in the case of the handbag. I told him I wanted to trace the Harcourt family. Normally he would have told me to close the case at this point.

Jack or should I say the chief was just as curious to find out its secret.

The Harcourt Family had moved to the outskirts of Eastbourne. I set off to find out the history of the handbag and with any luck the name of the spirit that had possessed it.

Their new home was similar to High Firs; so they still had stacks of money to afford a country home. The big wrought iron gates, long winding drive and endless sweeping lawns were nothing less than spectacular. At first glance, I thought the property was a castle as the first thing that struck me was the turrets along the edge of the roof.

As I pulled up outside the front door another car pulled up behind mine. I locked my car and a middle age man approached me from the car behind.

"Can I help you? I am the owner of this estate."

"I am chief inspector Peter Stewart and I take it you are Mr. Harcourt?"

"Sorry no, I am Adrian Seymore Mr. Harcourt is renting my coach house up the other drive next to the main gates."

As I arrived at the Coach House I spotted a man sitting at a garden bench reading a book. The man was in his late forties sporting a pipe, moustache and dressed in a loud jumper and golfing trousers. The man never took his head out of the book even when I stood next to him he still ignored me.

"Hello, are you Mr. Harcourt?" I asked and felt an instant dislike for the man who looked smug and arrogant.

"What do you want and what makes you think I am this Mr. Harcourt?"

"Your landlord confirmed you were, I would like to ask you some questions about High Firs."

"Blasted reporters, clear off before I give you a thrashing."

"Assaulting the Chief Inspector of police is strongly frowned upon so Mr. Harcourt unless you want me to arrest you, co-operate."

"I didn't realise, only you're not in uniform. What do you want to know?"

"I understand you left a large old trunk in the attic at High Firs."

"What about it? You can hardly call it fly tipping, there was some good stuff in it, am I supposed to get rid of it?"

"All I want to know about is the handbag, the black leather one with the ruby red velvet lining, who it belonged to and why it was left?"

"That belonged to my wife as did the rest of the contents in the trunk; I don't see your interest in it unless you think it was stolen."

"You had a fatality before you sold High Firs, was that your wife?"

"No that was the daily help and she was accused of stealing my wife's diamond ring. The police arrested her but had to let her go, mainly because they never found the ring."

"How did she die and why did you think she took the ring?"

"She was the only one apart from me and my wife in the house and when she was released after being questioned unbeknown to me she had turned up at the house. It was dark when I arrived home and I never saw her until it was too late, she died instantly the coroner told us."

"What was the woman's name? Moreover, if you have the address she lived at before the accident it would help. Oh! By the way where is your wife?"

"What is all this? My wife cleared off. The Daily's name was Celia Kent and lived at 14 Riverside court, so if that's all."

With that he stood up, threw his book on the garden bench and stormed off into the

Coach House. I had an eerie feeling Celia
Kent was trying to tell me something, if the
handbag is possessed, she must be the one,
but why, I had to find out.

Before returning to the station, I
called at 14 Riverside Court in case she had
any family still living there.
I got no answer. The head of neighbour
hood watch was opening their front door. If
I needed any information about any of the
neighbours this old woman was the one to
come to, yes; even special branch would
snap her up.
Mrs. Kent had a son still living in the flat
but he worked all the hours he could owing
to the grief he felt since his mother died, so
the old lady said. The old woman's name
was Miss Ethel Pelling with a memory like
an Elephant, it seemed Mrs. Kent had a
frequent visitor, mainly just after her son
had left for work and yes you guessed it; he
had a moustache and smoked a pipe. Miss
Pelling claimed that Alice Kent was as
honest as they come and was devastated at
the accusation that she had stolen the ring.
The man picked her up for work and
brought her back and Miss Pelling claimed
he returned some evenings and she could
hear Mrs. Kent in distress.

After thanking Miss Pelling I wrote my phone number down; just in case she remembered anything that could be of further use to me. I left and headed for the police station.

At the station I gathered six constables together and gave them a description of Mr. Harcourt. I then sent them to call on all the jewellers in the area to see if he had sold one of them the ring. I also gave them a description of the ring the insurance company had faxed through who had insured the diamond ring.

I was concerned about Mrs. Harcourt as I was sure Mrs. Kent's death was no accident and she may have had the same fate. The Chief would know who was sent to High Firs that fateful day so I called on him. I needed the case files so I could try to get to the truth.

Lucky for me the Chief had been involved in the case as he was still a sergeant at the time. He had been suspicions about Mrs. Kent's death and had taken an instant dislike to Mr. Harcourt when he interviewed him, just as I had.

At the time the police had not known of his involvement with Mrs. Kent.

The missing ring had been valued and insured for £27400. This was a strong motive but why kill his lover? My first concern was for Mrs. Harcourt so the Chief made it top priority.

I decided to go to the main post office to see if she had left a forwarding address for her mail, she had but it was c/o Mr. T Glover, 18 Brewery Towers, Hoppers Lane. I decided to pay Mr. Glover a visit. I felt quite sad when I saw the old brewery had been turned into apartments; The British way of life was gradually being wiped out. There was no answer from the door entry system so I tried other apartments until I got a response. Apartment 4 answered and was reluctant to give me access until I told her I was from the police. After I held my identity card up at the window she opened the main door, the woman introduced herself as Mrs. Funnel and confirmed a woman had recently moved in with Mr. Glover. I felt relieved that she was alive and I could get some vital clues to what really happened at Tall Firs. Apparently both leave before 8am and return about 5.20pm. As it was 4.40pm I told Mrs. Funnel I would wait for their return, she seemed excited I was a chief inspector and invited me in for a coffee.

I started feeling a bit uneasy when she kept on inquiring if I was married or involved with anyone. She was attractive but not what you would call pretty; if I was unattached I may have struck up a friendship. When I told her I was very much in love with my fiancée her chirpiness seemed to diminish; she told me that she had split up with her husband over his excessive drinking and gambling and was now divorced.

It was about 5.40pm when Mrs. Funnel went to her window and declared they were home as she had heard their car and after thanking her for her hospitality I went to wait for them at his flat.

The lift was opposite the flat and when it opened I noticed they had similar features, both with light brown hair and had the same type of expressions. I introduced myself and was reluctantly invited in. Mr. Gunter was her brother and they both worked in the same office block, they had kept in touch and seemed very close which was nice to see. She told me that when she had approached her husband about her suspicions concerning him and Mrs. Kent he lost his temper, hit her and then stormed out. She said she called her brother who came straight over to pick her up and take her back to his place and left her husband a note saying she would have them both in court so the truth would come out about his adultery. She was unaware that Mrs Kent had gone to the house that night and thought she may have turned up there to try to convince her nothing was going on, or had information about the ring as she had been dismissed. I on the other hand thought Mr. Harcourt had used the opportunity to get rid of Mrs Kent, without her there would be no proof. It was when I asked her if she would miss Tall Pines and she remarked that she had felt cut off being so far out in the sticks it hit me. Mrs. Kent never had a car so how did she get there? Apparently Mr. Harcourt always picked her up and took her home, so how did she get there that night

Mr. Harcourt claimed he arrived home in the dark and Mrs. Kent stepped out in front of his car from the darkness.

"Mrs Harcourt; the reason I reopened this case is down to your handbag you left in the old trunk in the attic."

"I brought all my belongings with me and as far as I know, that includes all my handbags."

"The handbag in question is a black leather one with ruby red velvet lining. Being such an expensive one I wondered why you left it behind."

"My husband bought that for Mrs. Kent one Christmas but how did it get in the attic? she loved that bag. I don't blame her for what happened she was a lonely sort but soon fell under my husbands charms. The day my ring disappeared was the last time I saw her with that bag."

"Let me tell you what I think happened, your husband stole your ring and put it in Mrs. Kent's handbag. When she realised what he had done she refused to keep the bag and wanted him to return the ring. Going by what I have learned about Mrs Kent she never had an affair with your husband but fought off his advances, she must have gone to your home that night to tell you what had been going on and your husband killed her."

"The poor woman, it all makes sense now, I think your right because she always looked at him with an annoyed expression."

"I can't arrest him on speculation, I need proof which I hope to get when our officers trace the ring. The handbag is possessed by Mrs. Kent's spirit and when a woman puts something valuable in it, it disappears and reappears in the man's jacket; do you think she is trying to tell us something?"
Mrs. Harcourt burst into tears.
"Would it be possible to have her handbag to remember her by? The poor woman how could he do that to her?"
"The bag actually belongs to the new owners of High Firs but she wants to see the back of it so I will see what I can do."
I left my card and headed off to try to catch Mrs. Kent's son at home.

My luck was in as I could see a light on in the flat. The front door was slightly ajar and the lock had been forced, quietly I entered the flat and hearing a noise from the bedroom I peered in to see Mr. Harcourt removing a drawer from the dressing table then reach into the opening.
I watched silently as he removed a small piece of cloth that had been stuck to the back of the opening. He put it in his jacket pocket before replacing the drawer.
"I take it that is the ring you stole from your wife Mr. Harcourt?"

He panicked and threw the dressing table stool at me before trying to rush past.

I took great delight in swinging him round hard against the bedroom wall and handcuffing him. As I did a man appeared in the hall and demanded to know what was going on.

"You must be Mr. Kent, I am Chief Inspector Stewart and this man is Mr. Harcourt. He has just broken into your flat to recover the ring your mother was accused of stealing."

"I know who he is; he kept pestering my mother to have an affair with him, you creep you never had the guts to come here when I was at home you waited until I had left for work. Hang on Inspector, what do you mean he recovered the ring?"

Before I had chance to stop him Mr. Kent lunged forward and punched Harcourt in the face, blood poured out of his nose and down his shirt.

"Back off Mr. Kent or I will have to arrest you, get me a towel quickly."

Mr. Kent brought a towel and I re-handcuffed Harcourt's hands in front of him and I gave the towel to help stop the blood from his nose.

"I will have you up for assault you maniac, you'll be sorry for that."
Shouted Mr Harcourt.
"It's your word against his Mr. Harcourt and you haven't any witness.
"You injured your nose when you attacked me while resisting arrest. Mr. Kent can verify that, can you confirm that Mr. Kent?"
"Yes that's exactly how he hurt his nose Inspector I can testify to that. I hope he gets done for breaking and entering."
"Partly but the main thing is murder and the proof is in his pocket."
Reaching in his pocket I pulled out the piece of cloth and revealed the ring. I then reached into his inner pocket took out his wallet and wrote down his credit card details.
"Phone a locksmith and get him here straight away to secure your front door. Pay for it with these details off Mr Harcourt's credit card, he can pay as he did the damage and here is my phone number, if there are any problems give me a ring anytime at all."

At the station I booked him for murder and hoped I could make it stick, there was no problem making the theft of the ring stick but Mrs. Kent's murder might be a problem.

After writing my report I decided to unlock my drawer and try something with the handbag. It was a long shot but I took it to Mr. Harcourt's cell and inserted the ring in it and when I opened it again it was gone, I looked in his pocket and there it was.

"What's going on; how did you do that? I must be dreaming."

"That was Mrs. Kent and I will leave this handbag along with Mrs. Kent's spirit in your cell last thing tonight."

"I never believed in the supernatural not until this handbag that you bought Mrs. Kent opened my eyes, she must have had it with her the night you killed her, that's why you put it in the loft; you ran her down but forgot about her handbag and you found it after the body was removed."

"Try and prove it, you think you are so smart, tell me how the ring was in her bedroom if I stole it."

"You went to see her after your wife accused you of having an affair and you put the ring in her handbag before you drove her home, you made some excuse to get her out of the room and that is when you hid the ring. When she was accused of stealing the ring she guessed you had taken it and was going to let her take the rap. She said she would tell your wife everything. You drove her to your home on that night in the pretence that you would own up to your wife, the real reason was to silence her."

"Spot on; No wonder they made you a Chief Inspector. I did kill her but there is no way of proving I gave her a lift that night."

"I have just recorded our conversation and as whether or not you drove her that night I may have the perfect witness. Miss Pelling may have seen you pick her up that night."

I phoned directory inquiries and got her number. She had indeed heard them quarrelling that night and seen them drive off.

Mr Harcourt was convicted on 1st degree murder. After the trial I picked up the handbag from my desk and thought I would give it to Mrs Harcourt as promised. I took one last look inside the handbag, to my surprise something had appeared rather than disappeared. Inside was a key ring in the shape of two shaking hands, inscribed. [**AT REST A.K.**] I have it to this day and always have an open mind no mater how strange things seem.

As Promised, I gave the bag to Mrs. Harcourt who put it in a glass case.

My fiancée Gracie complained that we had become passing ships in the night since I started this case. I agreed and took two weeks holiday to take her to Jersey for a long weekend. We spend the rest of the time at home.

Paris would have been nice but so would the money to pay for it, still we had a wonderful two weeks. The cases I stumbled on along the way dealing with the handbag were handled in my absence.

When I get another weird or extraordinary case I will be back.

So Long For Now

Chief Inspector Peter Stewart